Thorazine Dreams

Vic Kerry

This one is dedicated to Gramps and Gran.

Contents

Red Teeth

Dr. Stanford stood outside the backdoor to the emergency department taking the last drag off his cigarette. The moon hung full in the sky just over the tree line of the small pine copse that bordered the back of the hospital. On a night like tonight, he was happy to get a chance to suck down a Marlboro. Another would be nice to take the edge off. He glanced at his watch. The moonlight was bright enough that he could see the dial. Five minutes remained in his fifteen-minute break, enough time for another smoke. The soft pack with gold lettering on it had two cigarettes left when he bumped another out. Before it got to his lips, the back door flung open.

"We need you back in here." Meredith, the charge nurse, poked her head out of the opening.

"Let me finish this cigarette."

"You've not started it, and we're swamped. Just had another trauma."

Stanford shoved the unlit smoke into his lab coat's pocket. He popped a mint into his mouth and headed back into the ER. The noise of the machines and rushing staff assaulted his senses as he stepped inside. The night had been hectic since his shift had started, typical for a full moon. Most of his residency had been spent on the day shift. This was his first job as a *real* doctor. Night shift was the only position he could get, but it had proven exciting and tonight wouldn't be any different.

He followed Meredith back to the nurse's station. She reached over the counter and grabbed a metal clipboard with several colored pages. He glanced over the case load.

One of the worst things about working in the emergency department was you never knew what might walk in.

"I don't see a name on here."

"John Doe," Meredith said. "He apparently has some mental trouble or delirium or something."

"How is that a trauma?"

"He's covered in blood and can't tell us why. Might be a head injury."

"Any visible source of bleeding?"

"I don't know. I didn't do the triage, and they wanted him in here quick. Cops brought him. They said if you need them they could come back, but apparently, they're having a wild night too."

He looked at the bed number and headed to 2B. A nurse stepped out from the curtain. She held a tray with various blood-gathering implements on it. A few pairs of gloves dangled from the tray. Stanford grabbed a pair and pulled them on. He pushed back the curtain enough to step into the cubicle-like room. A man sat on an inclined bed. Dark stains that must have been blood covered his black T-shirt. The stains on his beat-up jeans were definitely blood. His beard looked as if it hadn't been trimmed in a long time. Wild hairs stuck out everywhere like some kind of animal.

"What's happened to you?" Stanford asked.

"This isn't my blood." The man's words came out fast and anxious. "I tried to tell them that, but they didn't want to listen to me."

"So whose blood is it?" He touched the man's arm and turned it over, looking for some kind of wound.

"I don't know."

"What's your name?"

The man's head toddled around like a bird in a cage. He tilted it to one side and stared as if he didn't understand the question. "I don't know."

Stanford continued his examination. John Doe's neck bore no wound. His head showed no injury, although blood gummed strands of his hair together. He looked into the man's eyes. Something seemed *off* about them. The eyelids looked too small. Stanford stood away from the patient and watched him. When John Doe blinked, slits of his eyes remained visible. Now he took notice of his hands. The fingers curled under, giving his hands the shape of clubs on playing cards.

"What's the matter with your eyes?"

"I can see fine."

"Your eyelids don't meet when you blink. Close your eyes."

The man closed his eyes. Indeed white slits were visible between his eyelids. John Doe opened his eyes again and coughed. His lips pulled back his grizzled moustache revealing his mouth. The teeth were a reddish color.

"Part your lips, please," Stanford said.

John Doe pulled at his lips with his gnarled, bent fingers. Stanford leaned in for a good look. The front two teeth were completely orange-red. The canines were lighter in color but still that rusty almost blood color.

"I'm a werewolf," John Doe said.

The patient stated it as a matter of fact.

"What?" Stanford almost dropped his clipboard.

"The blood is from my victim. On the full moons, I have to eat human flesh. I need the blood. I crave it."

"There's no such thing as werewolves. I think you're having hallucinations or something. They took your blood a few minutes ago for testing. Have they gotten a urine sample from you?"

"Yes. I promise that I killed a woman and fed on her liver. The full moon does it to me."

"I'm going to step out and check on your lab results. I'll be back in a few minutes."

Stanford slipped back through the curtain. He laid his clipboard down on the counter. Everything seemed a bit disjointed to him. Crazy people always made him feel that way. He'd hated his rotation on the psychiatric floor back in school. Psych patients had no place in an emergency room.

Meredith stood behind the nurse's station.

"Have the labs for the patient in 2B resulted yet?" he asked.

"Blood work is still out, and I haven't sent the urine off yet," Meredith answered.

"Why not?"

"I wanted you to look at it before I did."

The nurse put a plastic up full of cranberry-colored liquid beside the clipboard. Stanford picked up the specimen jar and studied it. When held to the light, the liquid bordered on opaque, but he could still see through it. He sat on a stool behind the counter and swished the specimen. The only time he'd ever seen urine like this it contained huge amounts of blood or was from a chemo patient. It swished around with no hindrance or residual stickiness as he would have expected that amount of blood in urine to do. He unscrewed the lid and took a whiff. The acrid, sour smell of urine filled not only his nostrils but the area around him.

"Put that lid back on," Meredith said. "You'll stink up the whole place again. We just got that smell out of here."

"Go ahead and get some vials up to the lab. I want a drug analysis stat. Something's going on with that guy, and I need to know what he has in his system."

Meredith took the jar. She pushed a small vial into the hole on the lid. The reddish-purple liquid shot into the vial. "Can he still not remember anything?"

"Oh, no, he's remembered something very important. He says he's a werewolf."

The nurse cut her eyes at him. He knew exactly what she was thinking.

"I'll put in to get these back in fifteen minutes." She held up two of the vials.

"Good. I'm going to pull some silver bullets from the Pyxis, just in case," Stanford said half kidding. "You said the cops brought him in. Did they report anything to triage about him being found near a woman? He said he killed one and ate her liver."

"They said he was delusional," Meredith said. "Which is more than apparent."

Stanford went to the machine that dispensed medications. A few taps into the keyboard, and the drawer opened that contained a small medication vial with Geodon written on it. He took out the vial and a syringe and slipped them into his coat pocket. Tonight, they might be needed.

John Doe sat on the bed staring straight at the ceiling when Stanford came back into the cubicle. The patient looked at him. Something seemed different in his look than the one he received when he left. John Doe seethed.

"Those labs haven't resulted, but I thought I'd do a few more physical examinations."

Stanford examined the patient's arm that he hadn't looked at previously. Nothing looked out of the ordinary on the parts not covered by his sleeve. The doctor pushed it up to reveal the shoulder. A few raw red lesions pocked an area from the elbow up. He poked them, but the patient didn't flinch.

"How long have you had these places?"

"Don't know, a while." The words were clipped and angry sounding.

"Are there any others?"

"My legs are covered with them. They come up after I transform. I suppose it's from where my skin ruptures as I turn into the wolf."

Stanford put John Doe's sleeve down. He pulled the patient's pant leg up. Sure enough, more of the lesions were there. Large clumps of the man's leg hair were missing as well. If he had been a dog, Stanford would have diagnosed him with the mange. *Maybe John Doe really is a werewolf.* He knew better than that. If anyone knew he'd even considered that idea, they'd blame it on his inexperience and second guess his abilities. For a doctor starting out, that was the last thing he needed.

"You're not a werewolf. There is no such thing."

"There is, and I am one." John Doe spat as he spoke. A string of frothy salvia hung from his mouth. His lips seemed to have receded some, and the red teeth looked more prominent. "I can feel the moon getting ready to crest in the sky. I have to get out of here before something bad happens."

"Nothing bad is going to happen. You just need to calm down. I'm going to get a nurse to give you something to help."

"You'll regret it."

Stanford shook his head and slipped out of the cubicle. Meredith stood on the other side of the curtain. She handed him several sheets of paper. He looked over them. The first was the drug screen. John Doe was negative for every drug of abuse. The next few pages listed out blood-test results. The only abnormality was low iron.

"Anemia, red urine and teeth, lesions, psychosis, but no drugs in his system or sign of infections." He thought for a moment. "Give him ten of Haldol, two of Ativan and one of Cogentin, now. I'm going out to smoke again and mull this over. I'll be back in a few minutes. If he causes a ruckus, put him in soft restraints."

He walked through the busy emergency room back to the rear door. The night air hit him in a cool burst. The cigarette already hung from his mouth when the door closed. As he lit up, he looked up at the moon. It rose nearly to its apex for the night. The smell of smoke filled his nostrils, but not that of his own cigarette. This smoke was headier and richer. Across from him in the shadows, a cigar cherry glowed as orange as a harvest moon.

"Busy night?"

"It always is on a full moon," Stanford answered, realizing the cigar belonged to the hospital's medical director.

The other man stepped into the moonlight. A ring of smoke encircled him. He took the stogie from his mouth.

"What's the big thing tonight?" the other man asked.

"I've got a man in there claiming to be a werewolf. He wants me to discharge him before he turns."

The medical director nodded his head. The cigar's cinder bobbed like a warning signal. "Well, it is a full moon. Have you consulted psych?"

"I told the nurse to give him a shot of Haldol. He doesn't report a history of psych, but he doesn't really know who he is."

"Psychosis?"

"Obviously, and his teeth are red, and his urine sample looked like cranberry juice. He has lesions he claims come from sprouting wolf hair, and his fingers are gnarled under."

"Porphyria."

"What?"

"It sounds like porphyria. It's a genetic disorder with all those symptoms. It's very rare, a once-in-a-lifetime thing for an ER doc like yourself. You need to put that on your merit badge sash. A fantastic prize for someone just starting out."

"All the symptoms?" Stanford dropped his cigarette and stomped it out.

"Believe it or not, all of them, including believing he's a werewolf. Porphyria has been offered as an explanation for folklore about werewolves and vampires. Go back and ask him if sunlight hurts him. If so, you're dealing with porphyria."

Stanford let the name of the disorder rattle around in his mind. He should have remembered that from medical school. Surely one of his instructors would have pointed out the disease, especially around Halloween when it would be topical.

"I'll do that, right now."

"Let me know what happens. I'll be looking forward to your take on things."

Stanford didn't bother with any more niceties. The rhythm of the ER hadn't changed much in the few minutes he spent outside. Nurses rushed to and from different cubicles. He made his way back to 2B. John Doe no longer lay in bed. He sat up like someone had attached him to a steel rod, on high alert. The ropy muscles of his forearms flexed beneath his skin. His eyes darted back and forth.

"Have you calmed down any?" Stanford asked.

"Of course not. The moon is nearly at its peak. I can feel it in my bones. You need to let me out of here."

"Did the nurse give you a shot?"

"What's that going to do? It won't stop me from transforming." He scratched his arms.

"Please settle back onto the bed for me. I need you to answer a few more questions. If you can do that then I'll let you go."

John Doe snapped his head toward Stanford. His eyes remained wild. He nodded and settled back onto the bed. The muscles in his arm flexed and loosened as did his jaw muscles. Stanford regretted telling the man he could leave after answering the questions; he really needed psychiatric hospitalization. Stanford couldn't remember the last time he'd seen someone so paranoid and delusional.

"Ask away." The words strained through clinched teeth.

"Do you have sensitivity to sunlight?"

"What kind of stupid question is that? Of course I do. All werewolves do. Why do you think we only turn at night?"

John Doe's head twitched hard to the left. He scratched harder at his arm. Stanford instinctively slipped his hand into his coat pocket and grasped the bottle of Geodon. He wished he'd drawn it up before visiting the patient again.

"I think you have something called porphyria."

"Does that mean werewolfism?"

"In a way, yes, it does."

"About time someone believed me. Are you going to let me out before I spread this porphyria to other folks?"

"I'm going to get the discharge paperwork for you." Stanford lied to the man. He was going to call the psychiatrist and get this man admitted to the psych floor for evaluation. John Doe would find this out when he came back with three big orderlies. "It won't take me but a few minutes."

"You might not have that long." A string of saliva trailed from John Doe's top lip down his chin.

Stanford slipped out of the cubicle and back to the nurse's station. Meredith sat by the telephone.

"Has the shot worked on him?" she asked.

"No. He's worse. Get the on-call psych doctor on the phone for me, and call up three big orderlies. We're going to have to transport him to the psych floor."

Meredith punched some numbers into the telephone and handed the receiver to Stanford. He explained the situation to the psychiatrist, making sure to say he thought his patient had porphyria. John Doe was accepted immediately, and the psychiatrist recommended a shot of Geodon for good measure. Stanford was way ahead of him, having already drawn up a dose while waiting for psych to answer. Three large orderlies joined him.

Stanford slipped the syringe into his pocket and headed back to 2B flanked by the orderlies. He pulled back the curtain and stepped inside. Before he had a chance to say a word, John Doe jumped from the bed onto one of the orderlies.

The force of the attack knocked the orderly down and slammed Stanford into the bed. It rolled against the wall. The two other orderlies scrambled to grab John Doe. Stanford moved to regain his balance as he fished the syringe from his pocket and popped the cap from the needle.

"Hold him still, boys!" he said.

"He's bit me!" one of the orderlies yelled and let go of John Doe.

The patient shoved hard against the last orderly and sent him pirouetting through the curtain and into the hall. A loud clatter echoed out as the falling assistant took out a tray. Stanford took the moment of confusion to stab the needle into the patient's shoulder.

He pushed the plunger as John Doe flung his arm backward. The patient's hand caught Stanford on the chin. It knocked him away, and he lost his grip on the syringe. The patient turned. He snarled, and strings of saliva slung from his mouth. Stanford saw the savage wildness in his eyes, like the stare of a rabid animal.

Stanford struggled to his feet. He held his fingers in front of him like a cross, thinking that if it worked on vampires it might work on someone who thought they were a monster.

John Doe leapt, knocking him back on the floor. The searing pressure of teeth sank into Stanford's forearm. John Doe shook his head like a dog with a squirrel. Stanford felt a plug of flesh tear free. Splatters of blood pelted his face. Despite the blinding pain, Stanford pressed his fingers in a pressure point on the patient's neck. John Doe fell back, spitting out the chunk of forearm, but rallied. He growled and pummeled Stanford, who threw up his hands to block the blows—punches like that of a heavyweight. John Doe's boney fist landed solid on the side of Stanford's face. His vision began to gray out as his arms lost strength and fell. Another hard-thrown punch landed in the same spot. The gray went to black, and Stanford let a weak gasp escape as he jolted into unconsciousness.

***

Stanford stared up at the bright full moon as he smoked a cigarette. The ER was busy just like every other full moon night, but it didn't seem to bother him too much tonight. He finished his smoke and crushed it out underfoot before walking back into the bustling ER. Meredith met him at the nurse's station with a metal clipboard.

"What we got now?" he asked.

"Cops brought in a guy claiming to be a werewolf," she said.

"Oh really? This I've got to see. Which bed?"

"2B," she said.

"Why do we always put the werewolves in there?" he asked.

"Just luck I guess."

"You better come with me just in case," he said.

Stanford and Meredith walked into 2B. He pulled the curtain back and allowed the nurse in first. A skinny, homeless-looking man with track marks up his naked arms sat on the bed.

"So my nurse tells me you're a werewolf," Stanford said.

"That's right I need some Xanax before I attack someone."

"Really?" the doctor asked.

"Yeah."

"I think we have something better than that." Meredith smiled at Stanford, showing off her red teeth.

"Indeed," he replied, smiling back with his own toothy, red smile.

Best Offer

Jack stared out his window to the street below.

His neighbor, Louis, bumped into the hedges that divided his yard from the Langley's. He'd been trying to get into their yard all day, but the chest-high hedge kept him at bay.

Confounded by the hedge, Louis looked horrible. His skin hung loose from his bones. His once dark-black hair had streaks of gray, and he wore a suit that was little more than tatters.

"How long has Louis been doing that?" Helen asked. She peeped over Jack's shoulder.

"All morning," Jack said.

"He looks horrible."

"Yeah, pretty bad."

"Has he turned?"

"He's a zombie, just like Mrs. Craig."

Helen pushed her husband aside. She watched the zombie Louis while he continued to knock into the hedge. The small limbs tore bits of his tattered rags away.

"What do you think he wants?" Helen asked.

"Probably to eat the Langleys' little dog. He can probably smell where it marked its territory on the other side of the hedge."

"Why doesn't he just go around?"

Jack glanced at his wife as if she were a complete idiot. "He's a zombie, Helen. They aren't known for having high intellect."

"But Louis was a lawyer. Yale even."

"I guess *zombism* doesn't care about degrees." Jack grabbed his pump-action shotgun. "I guess I better deal with him before he eats somebody."

Jack opened his front door and stepped onto his stoop. He pumped a shell into the gun's chamber. Louis heard the sound and faced him.

"How you doing this morning, Louis?" Jack asked.

"Brains," Louis answered with a long drawl.

"That bad, huh? Well, maybe you'll feel better in Hell."

Jack aimed at Louis' head. As the zombie lurched toward him, he pulled the trigger. Bits of blood and brain matter landed on the lawn while the rest of the zombie body crumpled to the ground.

Jack walked to the hulk of flesh, but kept the barrel of the shotgun pointed at it as he approached. The gray-skinned fiend lay still, not even a twitch. Satisfied of his safety, Jack laid the shotgun on the ground and grabbed Louis by the feet. He dragged the carcass to the curb and dumped it into the gully on the side of the road where he burned dead leaves.

"You need some gasoline?" Randy Langley asked. Jack's neighbor walked around the hedge carrying a red gas can.

"Douse him with it," Jack said. "I got matches in my pocket."

"I'm glad you took care of him." Randy tossed the pungent fluid on Louis' body. "I was out of shells. I didn't want to leave Marge and the kids alone with him trying to get in."

Jack struck a match on the side of the box and tossed it on Louis. The body lit up with a whoosh. "Have you ever heard of a neighborhood so full of zombies?"

"Not in this part of town. We're thinking about moving," Randy said.

"You won't get anything for your house. No one is going to pay top dollar to live in Zombie Acres."

"It's either get out for what you can get or get eaten by an elderly neighbor. Think about it."

Jack laughed. "I will."

The two neighbors watched the body burn to make sure the flames didn't get loose and catch the rest of the neighborhood on fire.

***

The front door closed hard.

Jack looked up from his newspaper. He'd been reading about the rash of zombie transformations. The article stated that local health authorities had no leads for the outbreak.

Helen walked into the room. "Guess what?"

"They still don't know why all these zombies are popping up in our neighborhood," Jack said.

"No. The Langleys are selling their house, for best offer."

Jack shook his head and folded his paper. "I told Randy he wouldn't get anything for his house by selling it during this zombie nonsense. Some people just won't listen to reason."

"When are we going to sell?"

"When all this zombie mess is over."

"What if we turn into zombies?"

"That'll be the day." Jack laughed and stood. "Where have you been?"

"Little Lisa Barnes just had tonsil surgery. I took her family supper. My secret recipe, you know."

Jack walked to the wet bar and poured bourbon into a tumbler. He mixed it with some water from the tap.

"You don't think jerk chicken might be a little spicy for a kid who just had throat surgery?" He held an empty glass toward Helen.

"I'll have the same," she said. "I thought about the spices. I cut them by a half."

Jack mixed her a bourbon and water and brought it to her. They both took long drinks. He carried his to the window.

A gray, old woman in a flowered nightgown and fuzzy slippers crept down the street.

"Old Mrs. Norris is one now," Jack said.

"Poor old thing," Helen said.

"I guess there'll be another house up for best offer."

****

Jack raked his front yard.

The autumn leaves built up nearly every day now. It was a common hazard of living in his neighborhood. He piled the leaves next to the hedge that separated his house from what used to be the Langleys. Their house sold about three weeks after it went up for sale. Since then, Mrs. Norris' house sold for a bargain price, as did the O'Malley's and the Jones'. Nearly every house in the subdivision was sold or emptying.

"You thirsty?" Helen strolled up the sidewalk carrying an empty casserole dish. "Just got back from Harriet's. She gave me back my dish from the supper I made for her."

Jack leaned on his rake. The orange and yellow leaves piled around his feet. "I could do with a highball. They're always best for raking leaves."

"You know ... I've not gotten my plate back from the Barneses yet."

"I didn't know you'd carried them more food."

"Lisa liked the Caribbean chicken so much while she was sick that I took another plate. This time the full recipe."

Jack stepped away from his pile. He took out a box of matches and lit one. He tossed it into the leaves. They flamed.

"You say the Barneses got the full recipe? I guess you'll be getting that plate back any day now." He raked more leaves onto the fire. "How about that highball?"

Helen went inside. Jack leaned on his rake and watched the flames curl the leaves to ash. The pile of leaves was like his neighborhood; soon nothing would be left. Only two houses other than his and Helen's still had families in them.

Helen returned with his highball but stopped short. The highball glass slipped through her hand and shattered on the sidewalk. "Jack!"

He turned. Max Barnes, gray and tattered, slinked down the street. His mouth dripped with bloody gore, and he carried the severed head of a little girl in his hand. Jack recognized Little Lisa, blanched and drained of blood.

"Get inside," he said to Helen. She didn't move. "Go on, before he sees you."

Max started toward Jack. Helen finally screamed and ran inside. Jack fumbled in his pocket and brought out a .38 caliber Derringer.

"How's it going, Max?" he asked.

"Brains."

"So did you take care of your wife, too?"

"Brains."

Max dropped the girl's head. It made a sick, cracking noise on the pavement.

"I'll take that as a yes," Jack said.

He popped both bullets into Max's skull. The zombie fell over, board stiff. Jack pocketed his gun and dragged the body onto the burning leaves. He raked more of autumn's droppings onto the body to build the fire. Eventually the clothes caught aflame.

"Is it safe to come out?" Helen yelled from the door.

"Yeah."

She walked out and stood beside Jack. He leaned on his rake watching the corpse burn. The smoke curled green and stank of burning, rotting flesh. Jack pulled a cigarette from his shirt pocket and lit it.

"Looks like another best offer house," Jack said. "I guess that supper you cooked for Harriet was full recipe?"

"Yup."

"I guess we'll have her house soon. At best offer rates, too." Jack tossed his cigarette into the fire. "What's for supper tonight?"

"Caribbean chicken," Helen said with a smile, "without the jerk spice, of course."

"That's my girl."

A Cat Named Hercules

Bart looked at the orange tabby sitting on the curb across from his apartment. He'd noticed it there for several days. It stared at him from beside the fire plug. Bart mentioned it to Mrs. Keifer, his neighbor. She'd seen the cat walking around the neighborhood too, which made Bart feel better. If she saw the tabby, it was real, and he wouldn't need a hospital visit or med adjustment.

Bart's stomach growled. He went inside his apartment to fix supper. He kept his front door open to let a mild southern breeze flow through his small apartment. It needed an airing out anyway. Bart didn't worry about someone walking in unnoticed because the kitchen, dining room, and living room were one in the same.

Bart took a Swanson chicken dinner from the freezer. He unwrapped it and placed it in his oven like every Friday night. When he turned around and walked to his stoop, the cat sat at his feet.

"Hello," Bart said. "What are you doing in here? I didn't invite you."

The cat blinked, wiggled his whiskers, and licked his chops. Bart stepped around him. The tabby followed. When Bart sat in the chair on his stoop, the tabby plopped down and stared.

"I don't have anything for you. You look healthy. Why don't you go back to your master?"

"I don't have a master." A deep voice resonated.

Bart looked around for the man who had spoken. He saw no one, just the cat sitting at his feet, blinking and wiggling his whiskers.

"Did you say that?"

"No." Cat lips moved. "It was my ventriloquist's dummy."

His striped tail stood over the cat's head. The tip bent over like a hook.

"We're dealing with a real bozo here?" The voice was cartoon-like.

"I think I need to take my pills early," Bart said to the cat. "They've worn off."

"No, they haven't. I'm as real as you are. Pet me and see."

Bart reached down and touched the silky fur. The cat purred and rubbed himself against Bart's leg, who sat up after realizing the reality of his talking tabby.

"What do you want from me?"

The cat looked up. "Right now, I'm hungry."

"I don't have any cat food."

"Go to the store. A can of Friskies is only thirty-three cents."

"I'll have to walk, and my dinner will burn."

"Go after you eat. I can wait that long. I'll be on the couch." The tabby flourished his tail and trotted to the door. He looked over his shoulder. "You can call me, Hercules."

***

Bart stumbled through the dark and dumped two Dollar General bags onto his table. He flipped on the light. The fluorescents hummed to life.

"Did you get the stuff?" Hercules' voice boomed from behind Bart.

He jumped. "You scared me."

"Did you get the stuff?"

"Of course, I did. You sent me to get it. Everything's just like you wanted."

"Good, dig me out some chicken, and feed me."

Bart rummaged through a bag and found a tin of chicken-flavored cat food. Hercules purred and rubbed himself against his leg. Bart emptied half of the can into a saucer before placing it on the floor. Hercules ate.

Bart put away the cans and set up the litter box in his bathroom. He walked back into the living room to watch TV. Hercules sat perched on the sofa, licking his chops after supper. Bart sat down beside his cat and stroked him.

"Stop that," Hercules said. "When I need stroking, I'll tell you, capiche?"

Bart turned on the TV and began watching the news. Hercules cleaned himself.

***

"Bart." The baritone echoed from the distant darkness. "Bart, wake up. I have something I need you to do."

The voice grew louder inside the vast blackness. The repeating words boomed. Bart opened his eyes to the darkness. His gaped mouth had fur in it. He tried to spit, and Hercules retreated, resting on Bart's chest.

"What do you want? It's two in the morning."

"I know what time it is. It's time for you to feed me. I'm hungry and want some dry food."

"At daylight," Bart rolled over.

A paw with claws extended touched his nose. "No, now. It's an order."

"You're a cat. I'm a man. I outrank you."

"I can do things to you that'll make you fear for your life."

Hercules' claws slid down Bart's face to his chin. They scraped the skin enough to let Bart know they were there. Then Hercules stretched out toward Bart's mouth, making his front legs spread in a V on both sides of Bart's chin. The cat's eyes grew large and iridescent. Hercules' nostrils flared as he inhaled a deep breath. Bart felt the air seep from his nose and mouth. He gasped to regain it, but it slipped from him as though his lungs collapsed as the air sucked out. His chest burned; his vision dimmed. He tried to scream but could only muster a squeak. With his last bit of strength, he patted his hand on Hercules' hind end.

The cat sat up. His eyes quit glowing, and air refilled Bart's shriveling lungs. He gasped and panted.

"You've never heard that a cat can steal your breath?"

Bart nodded in agreement.

"Maybe you won't argue with me anymore. Get me some Meow Mix, now."

***

Bart spent the next two days waiting on Hercules hand and foot. He woke up at Hercules' every whim. They watched what the cat wanted on television, and even walked through the neighborhood when Hercules decided he needed fresh air. The whole time the cat threatened to take Bart's breath away again if he did not do exactly what he was told.

Bart woke up on Monday morning at 5 a.m. Hercules lay curled on the foot of his bed. He went to the bathroom, took a shower, and dressed to go to day-treatment at the mental health center like he did every Monday. He slipped through his bedroom. Hercules still slept in a ball on his bed.

Bart made himself eggs for breakfast. He plopped them on some toast and sat down at the table.

"What are you doing, Bart?" Hercules leapt up beside the plate.

"Having breakfast."

"Why are you up so early? You usually don't rouse until I get you up."

"I've got day-treatment today at the mental health center."

Bart bit into his sandwich. A crumb of egg fell onto the table. Hercules crouched, sniffed and gobbled it up. He licked his chops as he looked Bart in the eyes.

"So you're just going to leave me here all day by myself?"

"I was going to leave the radio on for you."

"Oh, that's supposed to suffice. What if I get hungry?"

"I'm going to give you breakfast and leave you some extra dry food."

"What if I get thirsty?"

"I'll leave water, too."

"What if I need the bathroom?"

"Your box is fixed in my bathroom."

"What if I get lonely?"

"I'll only be gone four hours."

Bart put his plate in the sink and washed it. He could feel Hercules watching him. He finished washing his dish and took a can of cat food out of the cabinet. He opened it and spooned it into Hercules' bowl. He got out the dry food and poured a heaping pile on a saucer. Bart turned back to his feline housemate.

"See, I've got everything set up."

"You can't go."

"I have to. I'm on an outpatient commitment. If I don't go, they'll send me back to the hospital, and then I'll have to go to the state asylum. You'd be stuck here trapped in my apartment."

"That won't happen. I won't let it," Hercules said with an air of authority.

"You can't overrule the state, and I'm not going back to the asylum if I can avoid it."

Bart gathered up a few things he needed. He walked to the door, pocketing the door key.

"I'll be home this afternoon."

"If you walk out that door, I will kill you when you come back."

"Sure you will."

***

Bart couldn't focus on the group topic. He ruminated over Hercules' threats.

He's going to kill me.

The thought was so clear, so distinct. Other times when Bart felt paranoid, he'd either heard the wicked voice telling him that someone was out to get him, or he felt quiet dread. This was different. He could not get the idea off his mind. When group ended, Steve, the therapist, called him aside.

"Bart, you look a little bit preoccupied. What's going on?" Steve asked.

"I was thinking about my cat."

"When did you get a cat?"

"Friday. He wandered up and welcomed himself into my house. He's been demanding food and undivided attention ever since."

"Sounds like a cat to me," Steve said cheerily. "What's to worry about?"

"He's going to kill me."

"How do you know that?"

"He told me so, and he tried Friday night. He took my breath away."

"That's a wives' tale. Cats can't really do that."

"Tell that to Hercules. He told me if I came to treatment he would kill me when I got home. He's an evil cat, and the only thing I can do to stop him is kill him."

"Maybe you should call the humane society and let them have him."

"He'd escape and stalk me until he could do me in. He's an evil kitty."

"Are you sure this isn't some hallucination or paranoia?"

"No. Mrs. Keifer, my neighbor, can see him."

"Can she hear him?"

"He's never talked to her."

"What about going to the hospital again for a few days to get your meds fixed?"

"I've spent enough time there. Plus, the doctor told me if I went back, she's sending me to the asylum."

"Let's think about it."

Bart darted out of the group room. He ran from the mental health center to his apartment in fifteen minutes, half his usual time. Hercules was nowhere to be found. Bart crept into the kitchen and grabbed a knife.

"Hercules, I'm home. Where are you at?"

Nothing moved or made a sound. Bart crept back into the living room and then his bedroom. Hercules was not on the bed or under it. He peeked into the bathroom hoping to catch him using his box. He found only fresh cat urine.

"Where are you, kitty? Here kitty, kitty."

A loud bang rattled the front door. Bart jumped and hurried into the living room, gripping the knife tighter.

"Bart, this is Steve. Let me in."

"Not until I fix my problem."

"I'll give you until three," Steve said. "One."

Bart looked under the couch.

"Two."

He looked under the recliner.

"Three."

The door burst open as two cops stormed in. Bart turned to them still holding his knife.

"He's got a knife," one of the cops yelled.

"Drop it!" the other pulled out his pistol.

Bart dropped the knife on the floor and raised his hands. The first cop grabbed his arms and handcuffed them behind Bart's back.

"You've got to believe me. My cat is trying to kill me."

"Take him to Regional Hospital. They're expecting him," Steve said.

The officers put Bart in their car. He stared out the window, watching Steve close his front door. Hercules scuttled out. Steve picked him up. Bart could read Steve's lips: *What a sweet kitty.*

The Night Sputnik Spoke

I've worked for the KGB since June 12, 1945. I met my first comrade after marching into Berlin. He introduced me to the ideas of V. Lenin and taught me the power of the proletariat. After a brief education in communism, I became a secret Marxist disciple and agreed to work with the Soviet government to overthrow the materialistic United States. After my tour in Germany and the dropping of the big ones in Japan, I was sent stateside and began my work for the Motherland. All went well until the Feds got wind of my obedience to the "Red Menace." I began talking to myself and tricked them into believing that I was mad. They put me in this asylum where I've spent the last seven years.

Over the grueling time, I've been subjected to all kinds of mind control. The psychiatrists were no doubt working with Hoover and his G-men to try and break me. So far, so good. I hadn't revealed anything of my nature as a spy until a few days ago. A major watershed moment occurred, that night I heard a very distinct message from my Soviet comrades. Beep ... beep ... beep... It was the sound of Soviet triumph, the radio emission from Sputnik.

After seven years of being in a gulag of dimwits and madmen, my Soviet brethren had sent me a message of hope. Before leaving Berlin, my connection had told me of a secret code that KGB spies used to communicate so that only fellow KGB men would know what was being said. The night the orderlies had all the delusionals sitting in the common room listening to the world news on the radio, I heard the message beeping from high above my head in the inky blackness of space.

"Our fellow Soviet brothers and sisters, the Motherland has succeeded. We have overcome the oppression of the imperialistic West. Our secret brothers waiting for the moment to attack… *Attack!*"

I jumped to my feet and shouted obedience in my best Russian. Then the orderlies pushed me back down in the chair and threatened me with the mind control serum they kept in their glass syringes. I sat quietly watching the other madmen drooling from the corners of their slack jaws, not realizing that the world would soon be under the regime of true equality and comradeship. I turned in earlier than usual, to keep the overeager orderlies from filling my backside with a mega-dose of sedatives.

In my room, I kept the light out. I had the luck of being institutionalized longer than my other roommates, which made me the alpha dog. I got the bed by the slit of a window. I kept my back to the door, and my eyes peeled to the night sky. The stars showed brightly even with the obscuring of the wire-reinforced glass. I saw Mother Russia's triumph drift through the still night air. The moving star of Earth's first artificial satellite. It beeped out the time of victory was upon us. The time of the worldwide red revolution was coming, and it would be broadcast around the world on Sputnik.

I couldn't sleep. My eyes would close but only momentarily. I felt as though I had drunk fifty cups of coffee. My mind raced with the thoughts of what glorious jobs I would have and what title and award I'd be given for enduring the torture of the Americans in their nut house. They would give me the highest commendation for loyalty. I watched the sky until the first red rays of morning broke on the horizon. A new, glorious, red day dawned.

When the wake-up sounded out through the hallways, I queued first in line for the head. I stood first in line for the breakfast of bacon and grits, for medication, and to get out into the yard to enjoy the new, glorious day. I hadn't slept a single wink but felt like a million rubles. Fresh air wafted the smell of October into my nostrils. The scent of the dusty leaves and leaf smoke floated around me. The sky seemed as far away as the patrolling satellite, clear and bluebird blue. A few wispy clouds drifted through the gem sky.

Big Bob, the giant of an orderly, had been given the job of airing us out that day. Of all the orderlies, I respected him the most. He didn't have all the brains, but he'd listen to me when I talked. He didn't treat me like I was off my rocker. He'd interject things that he knew about Marxism, and he, too, had marched into Berlin.

Big Bob stood nearly seven feet tall with broad shoulders. He had to duck and turn sideways to come in and out of the doors. His chest stuck out like a whiskey barrel. He didn't have a single hair on his head. If any of the other patients got too rowdy, the nurses sent for Big Bob. He could calm down a patient faster than any sedative shot.

One time a new guy came in. He was a skinny squirt who thought he was really something else. He had bashed his head against the walls while he was in some county jail and wound up in the nut joint. He came in whooping and hollering like a monkey. No one could do anything with him. He even broke the head nurse's thumb. After that, Big Bob came in. That wild monkey had been hitting every orderly and nurse that came near him. The next thing that nut knew Big Bob put him in a bear hug, turned him upside down and dangled him headfirst over the hard tile floor. Things settled down after that.

Everyone on the ward gave respect to Bob, and strangely enough, he gave respect back. He didn't have to be mean to intimidate. He had the girth for that, so he could be congenial to us. Oftentimes, he'd walk with me in the yard as we talked about how the poor were getting used by the capitalistic system of the West. He agreed that the poor don't always get the best in life, but he stopped short of thinking of himself as a socialist. He stated that he didn't fight the Krauts and the Gooks so that the "good ole" U.S.A. could go "pinko." I liked him anyway.

This day Big Bob and I sat on the cool ground watching the wispy clouds float by. We didn't say a word for a long time, but just admired the beauty of the new day in a now smaller world.

"What about those Russkies launching that metal bowling ball up there?" Big Bob pointed to the sky.

"Impressive."

"I'd never thought that the Pinkos would get a jump on us." He looked over at me with a broad grin over his dishpan face. "Maybe you're right about that Soviet superiority and comradeship you're always jawing about."

"Finally, you see things my way. You know it broadcasted a message last night."

"Really? I heard it beeping, but I didn't realize it was sending a message. Was it in Morse code?"

"Oh no, no, no," I shook my head. "It was a coded message that only members of the KGB located around the globe would know."

"So you're a member of the KGB?"

I had to sidetrack some here. I'd never told Big Bob about my real mission. He'd turn me over to the Feds for sure. He was all American, red, white and blue, Yankee Doodle.

"No, I just knew some members before landing in here. They'd told me about the secret messages."

"So what was it?" Big Bob asked.

"I don't know. I was never told the message; just that one would be broadcast when the Soviet triumph was upon us."

Big Bob wore a joshing smile on his face. It insulted me to the core. For all the respect he had given me, he mocked me at the moment of my greatest success. I didn't have time to say anything. The sky ripped apart.

A huge explosion roared out across the yard. Lunatics screamed as their paranoid delusions and voices yelled a variety of lies. I covered my head knowing what was happening. Big Bob jumped to his feet. He thought he knew what was happening too.

The Western world fell as the sky crashed before us. The Soviet missiles rained down nuclear death on the U.S. and her oppressive allies. The socialist revolution had begun in a glorious roar of atomic thunder. I waited to be dissolved in the heat of a nuclear reaction, but that didn't occur. The sky screamed again with a smaller explosion, and fire began to rain down. Drops of liquid inferno splattered on the yellowing grass of the yard. Dry patches caught alight and raced to more dry patches. Big Bob jerked me to my feet. The other loonies ran from the falling fire and brimstone hail.

"It's the apocalypse!" a paranoid schizo yelled before a wad of liquid fire landed on his shirt, setting him alight. He fell, rolling around to smother the flames.

Big Bob ushered the running people to the door that led back into the building. Fire engulfed the building. I brought up the tail. Several patients had fallen on the lawn, some dead from the impact of the falling sky. Others were too injured to go on.

As I stepped through the door into the common room, the earth shook. An explosion sent parts of the ceiling tumbling down. The windows shattered inward. Glass flew, burrowing into the patients who had been lucky enough to avoid the burning rain. Several shards plunged into the right side of my face. Then a fireball rolled across the lawn. The few souls left out there were fried like Friday's chicken lunch. The paint on the bricks bubbled from the heat.

As quickly as the punishing hell rain started, it ended. Before I was shuffled into the interior of the hospital, I glimpsed the lawn. The trees burned, the dead smoked, and what looked like metallic rubble dotted the scorched grass. The sky was still blue, and wispy clouds still raced along the path of the high altitude winds.

***

The population of the men's wing of the hospital was moved to the south wing. It hadn't been used regularly in a long time but was kept manageable. The men's wing had suffered a lot of damage during the fire storm. The upper floor and roof had smoke damage. The unit they moved me to was one that Dr. Kildare had run. He had been long gone, before my time, but when you're in an asylum and are marginally sane, you hear legends. He should have been a patient on the ward rather than run it. Dr. Kildare held wild social concepts about the superior race, much like the Krauts. He systematically killed his own patients in the very ward they stuck me in.

I think they had gotten wind of the message I had been sent by my comrades. I had a suspicion Big Bob told the administrator what we had been talking about before the sky fell.

The Feds instructed the administration to house me in this ward. Legends had it that the ghosts of the patients that Dr. Kildare euthanized still haunted the halls. Supposedly, those vengeful spirits had tossed him from a fifth floor window to the cement below.

This had to be it, because the G-men showed up not long after the firestorm. They came almost as quickly as the fire department. It wasn't just the FBI, but the military as well. I saw brass like I hadn't seen since Berlin. I saw at least two brigadiers, one Army, the other Air Force. Big Bob said that all the government men were there to investigate what happened.

"I overheard Dr. Lauder talking about it with Nurse O'Hare. He said that something had been spotted flying over on the radar. A few sabres went up and shot it down. He didn't say what it was, but it rained down on us that day," Big Bob told me.

"What was it, a MiG?"

"Never heard. I don't think Dr. Lauder had been told. Everybody is saying it was a UFO." Big Bob sounded as paranoid as one of the inmates.

"UFO," I couldn't help but scoff. "You don't believe in that nonsense, do you?"

"I don't know, but whatever exploded wasn't like any aircraft I've ever seen. I saw lots of them come down during my time in the army. I've seen our big bombers, Kraut fighters and bombers, Jap fighters, MiGs and sabres all hit the ground. None of them did what that thing did."

This conversation made me think. The message broadcast from Sputnik said the revolution had started. Had my comrades built some new secret jet weapon? Had they breached the stars with manned flight? My mind raced with the flurry of what ifs. I spent many a day and night mulling these things over. I spent so much time pondering this that I didn't realize what had started to happen.

On the third day of my mulling over the new Soviet weapons, Dr. Lauder ordered me a little cocktail of sedatives to slow me down. It did its job. I went down about four in the afternoon and rose a few days later. When I woke, I noticed something different about my ward mates.

Douglas MacArthur sat in an overstuffed chair staring out the window. That was the first thing I noticed. Doug never sat looking out the window. He had too much energy for that. He retook the Philippines at least three times a day. He just sat there looking at the rain-splattered windows, his mouth slack and his gaze focused on nothing. His color had turned an ashen gray.

"We had to give him the juice," Big Bob said, passing me as I spoke to Doug.

"The juice?"

"They ordered him to get one of those shock treatments. He didn't do so well with it. Must've fried his brains. He's been sitting there for the last day or so. Nurse O'Hare said he won't come back. Says she can tell by the lack of spark in his eyes."

I looked at his eyes; no spark. In its place, I saw deep horror. After our salvation from the firestorm, Doug and I had talked a lot about what had happened. He claimed he saw what crashed. He said it looked like a strange jet, larger than usual and breaking up as it approached the ground. The nose was red hot. He wasn't shy about talking. I think he even talked with a few of those military men. I, of course, lied and said I had seen nothing, even though I had seen the strange metallic pieces spread across the lawn. Poor old Douglas MacArthur said too much, and the Feds scrambled his brains for him. They weren't going to do that to me. I was too clever for them. My Russian friends made sure of that.

A few days later, Doug was gone. He just disappeared, and another patient was in the same shape he had been in a few days prior. Big Bob wouldn't answer my questions. He wouldn't even speak to me. Every time I saw Big Bob, he pushed a wheelchair with patients in varying degrees of catatonia toward the green metal door at the end of our ward. It had been Dr. Kildare's "mercy room." A sign on the door still bore the words: *No admittance. Authorized personnel only by order of psychiatrist.*

I caught glimpses of the patients as they wheeled by me after leaving the "mercy room." They never came out as well as they went in; some never came out. I had stopped recognizing the patients after a few days. My ward thinned out. The people being brought by Big Bob looked like they had been in the infirmary or nursing home. Each appeared to be a few days from death.

A horrible thought crossed my mind as I watched the goings-on without appearing to notice. We had all witnessed what had fallen from the sky. Even those who weren't on the lawn that day knew. Half of the hospital had caught on fire in some way. The government had come in to clean up. They were getting rid of the witnesses by frying our brains. They hadn't come for me yet, because they knew I was a KGB member. They either feared that my comrades would attack them if they harmed me, or they were torturing me by making me await my turn at the juice.

Big Bob stopped pushing decrepit old crazies down the hall. A skinny woman with tightly stretched skin began pushing them instead. She had dark circles under her sunken, dazed eyes. The skin on her face was stretched so tightly every sinew in her head twitched and strained when she grimaced. She came by my room every morning at 5 a.m.

before the wake-up call. I'd watch her out of the little window in my door. She would grin at me. It was a dreamy grin like patients had after getting the sedative cocktail.

On her empty return trip, I stopped her as she sauntered down the hall.

"What happened to Big Bob?"

The skeletal nurse grinned, stretching her facial skin even tighter over her jawbone. The blue veins became visible underneath the gray almost transparent skin. "He died."

"Died? Of what?"

"Blood problem." The nurse's voice sounded hollow as if her entire body was void of anything.

"Like hemophilia?"

"You might say that."

The nurse smiled another taut grin and walked away. I stepped back into my room. Big Bob had never mentioned being a hemophiliac. We had talked about a lot of problems. I doubted the nurse's story. I wished that I was able to contact my Russian comrades for advice. I'd not had to investigate things quite like this: A good friend was missing, a constant parade of patients going into the mercy room, but not coming out, and the corpse-like nurse mincing up and down the corridor in the mornings. She smelled like a corpse too, a sweet rotting odor. The answer lay in the mercy room. That's where everyone was going. I'd go to the room myself and see what was behind the door. I would wait until lights out because fewer eyes watched then. My KGB brothers would be proud.

"I'm going to find out what is going on here, for myself, Big Bob, and Mother Russia!" I yelled to the closed door and those behind it.

They gave me a shot. I awoke the next day in a padded room, strapped down as if I were being crucified. Filtered sunshine from a high skylight lit the bed. Leather restraints cut off the circulation to my hands. They tingled. Then I heard a noise coming from my left. I came more to my senses and realized that the breath from my mouth steamed. The noise to my left became louder. I turned my head, which was the only free part of my body. The door at my left was closed, but a greenish light seeped from its edges. The chilly air made the sound stronger. It sounded like a cat lapping up milk but much louder. The smell in the room smothered me. It was a rusty odor, very strong, mixed with a bittersweet medicinal smell. The slurping grew louder, the smell stronger, and I swooned.

I woke on the tile floor free of the restraints. I could see the door from before still closed and the weird light coming out of the cracks around it. The rusty, bittersweet odor had lightened. The sun had started to set so that room was dimmer. The slurping sound couldn't be heard. I scooted across the floor on my belly like we did in the war. I stopped when I could press my eye to the crack under the green-lit door. I could see into the next room. The corpse nurse lay topless on the floor. She stared at the ceiling. Everything in the room, including her, looked green in the smoky light.

A haunting sound echoed on the tile floor, the wet plopping noise of footsteps. I saw a reptilian webbed foot. Then the whole creature moved into view. It wasn't tall. The body had long hair like stripped feathers. Its bald head had large eyes with huge pupils. The snout-like mouth had two nodules at the jowl, and the nose was little more than slits, like that of a snake. The hair on his right flank had been peeled away and a large sutured line ran from what would be a knee to what would have been the groin, which testified to an injury.

It knelt over the topless nurse and puckered its mouth. Its breath wafted a reddish-orange smoke. The bittersweet smell began to seep through the crack I watched from. I held my breath, taking gasps only through the filter of my shirt. The vapors crept up my nose anyway. My brain detached from my head and floated around the room. Purple and green dots danced in front of my eyes like Russian ballerinas. This all grayed out, but I didn't swoon. The nurse settled back. The creature opened a mouth full of cat-like needle fangs and bit into the woman's left breast. Blood began to run out of the breast in several crimson streams. The creature leaned closer and between the lightly touching fangs, its tongue lapped out and brought the blood into its mouth. More orange smoke billowed from it. This time I could not ward it off and passed out.

I've been awake for an hour. The sun has started to come up, and it is pitch dark in the room, except for the light from underneath the door. The lapping noise continued after I awoke but has diminished as time passed. I suppose the nurse is dead, and her blood drank up. It seems Big Bob died of blood loss after all, just not anything congenital. I assume I am next. I don't know why else I'd have been put in this room.

As I've been writing my account in my best Russian on my T-shirt with my own blood (the only ink I have available and the less that thing will be able to suck out of me), I've figured out a few things. It seems the night my comrades sent the world a message of the dominance of the Soviet regime; they sent another message out: Here we are; come and get it. The firestorm of a week ago was the alien in the other room's spaceship crashing to earth. The government must've shot it down. It has since been feeding on the patients and staff. I hope that this information will help others, especially my comrades.

I smell that bittersweet smell. I think it is intended for me this time. Long live the revolution!

Thrill Kill

Sam's ancient Plymouth beater died at the far end of the old iron bridge three miles from home. He reached into his glove box and took out his wallet and .38 special. As he crawled out of the dark green Duster, he shoved the gun into his work coat's pocket and his wallet into the back pocket of his grease-spotted jeans. His work boots clopped on the pavement as he walked down the road toward the bridge. After a few days of early November rain, which left the air crisp and the leaves colorful, the water rolled high and muddy under the span. Sam slid his hand into the pocket that held the pistol as he stepped off the bridge. He kept the gun in his car because he often worked overtime into the evening and owl shifts. He had to go through some rough country to get home from the strip mine. Moonshiners and meth cooks hung out in the deep woods. No one ever knew what those dudes might do.

He walked past Creek Bank Road. The muddy rutted road followed the creek bank to a party area near an old cemetery where they said a lot of weird stuff happened. Sam remembered how he and his high school buddies would ride out there during the day to drink and smoke a doobie, but would head out as soon as the sun set behind the trees. Satan worshipers supposedly sacrificed blond-haired, blued-eyed virgins in that graveyard, and Sam had dishwater blond hair and happened to be have been a virgin back then.

The pistol grip sat in his palm. It felt a little bit childish, but you never knew what might pop up out there. Although he was pretty sure Satan wasn't too interested in him as a sacrificial lamb anymore. The coal dust on his face made him look as black as a demon burned in hellfire; the devil would probably think he was one of his own.

"Hey, pal."

Sam turned to the high weeds at the opening of the road. A man stood from a squat. He wore an army-surplus field jacket over a yellowed wife beater. Thin black tattoos twined around his neck. His beard had three days growth on it, and his eyes looked red. Sam gripped the pistol and walked on as if he didn't hear the man.

"I know you heard me. I just need a little money, man. I'm down on my luck."

"Aren't we all," Sam said.

"Right on, brother."

"I ain't your brother, and I suggest you move on down the road before you get hurt." Sam half turned and let the outline of his piece show through his coat's fabric.

He didn't have time to react before the loafer jumped up and ran at him. The scraggly man bowled him over. They hit the pavement hard. The gravel tore a hole in Sam's coat and shirt. His elbow scraped across the rocks. He hissed against pain of the pavement cutting into tender flesh. The loafer rolled them over and ended up on top. He punched Sam across the face.

Stars danced before Sam's eyes. The loafer shoved his hand into the coat pocket and pulled out the pistol.

"What we got here? A .38 special?" He rolled the cylinder out and looked the bullets over. "With wadcutter? Serious business."

"Give me that back." Sam tried hard to keep from sounding angry or scared. He didn't know if he had succeeded.

The loafer stood, straddling Sam. "I don't think so. What did you say your name was?"

"I didn't."

The cylinder locked into place, and Sam found himself staring down the barrel of his own gun. "I suggest a proper introduction."

"My name's Sam, and I'm walking home because my car broke down. My place is just a ways up the road. I'll give you my wallet and whatever. Just let me go. I got a wife and a kid."

"Well, Sam, they call me Gnat, 'cause you don't see me 'til I'm on you, and I'm annoying as hell. I don't think that wallet's going to cut it." He lowered the gun and held his hand out to help Sam stand. "I'm going to walk you home, and we're going to play a game."

"I don't like games." He allowed Gnat to help him to his feet. Arguing with those kind of people would be pointless; plus, Gnat had his pistol.

"You'll like this one. You see there are five bullets in the cylinder of this gun. If we pass five cars before you get home, then you're free. If we don't, I shoot you. How does that sound?"

Sam wanted to say *not good actually*, but he nodded. Gnat patted him on the back, and they started walking down the road.

He won't shoot me. He's just high and goofing off, Sam told himself, but the dryness of his mouth and the slight quaking of his hands didn't seem to agree with his thoughts.

They walked down the shoulder about a fourth of a mile before the first low hum of a car carried on the air. Gnat flipped the cylinder of the pistol in and out as they walked.

Sam clenched his jaws tight. His molars ached.

As the drone of the car engine grew louder, Gnat clicked the cylinder into place. He smiled at Sam, who could see that his teeth had black holes at their rims near the gum line—meth mouth. Sam worked with a few guys with the same grin. They smoked crank to stay awake during their shifts at the pit. Gnat probably smoked it because it was the only way he could get a daily thrill.

Sam and Gnat started up a rise in the road, canopied by the red and oranges of November leaves. A yellow Ford Fiesta crowned the hill. Sam didn't recognize the car. This old road didn't get used much anymore, so either the driver was lost or heading to Creek Bank Road to party with the likes of Gnat. Sam felt a twinge of anticipation in his gut. *He won't do it.*

The Fiesta passed. Gnat waved to the driver, then pulled the gun, aimed and fired. The old rusty, yellow Ford kept whining as it drove into the ditch. Breaking glass and crutching metal announced the extent of the damage.

"Alas, poor old Yorick, I knew him well, Sam."

Sam's mouth remained dry—drier than he ever thought it could get. His tongue stuck to the roof of his mouth as he tried to speak.

"That's not funny," Sam said.

"What? You agreed to this game, and I knew the guy. We partied all the time. He was a high school English teacher once. We called him Yorick 'cause *Hamlet* was his favorite play. He was heavy."

"I didn't agree to the game. You forced me."

Gnat leveled the gun at Sam's face. The barrel smelled of spent gunpowder.

Sam tried to swallow, but only dry wind blew down his throat. He grinned, his lips sticking to his teeth. "Just kidding."

Gnat lowered the pistol and nodded his approval. Sam began to think that his old adolescent fear of being sacrificed to Satan might come true after all. Gnat seemed like a man in cahoots with the devil, probably a prize stallion in Hell's barn.

They walked into the dying light of afternoon. Sam's house kept getting tenths of miles closer. Four bullets remained in the chamber. His odds of getting away weren't good with that many chances for Gnat to pop him.

They crossed a small bridge over a railroad track. The old boarded-up gas station came up on the right. The roof sagged from years of neglect. The community cemetery came into view, the first visible headstones tipping over the rise in the ground. A low hum came from down the road. The whine of this engine told the story of a newer and well-maintained vehicle. Sam knew it sounded much healthier than his old Duster and better than the doomed Fiesta of Yorick. A white sedan popped into view. He didn't know this one either. The car rolled toward them. Sam thought about throwing his hand up to wave off the car.

"Don't think about it," Gnat said as if he could read his mind. "It ain't worth it, man."

Sam didn't disagree. He had two miles to home, where he might have a chance to run for it and get inside. A 12-guage pump-action rested beside the front door. He would have no problem pumping off a few rounds at old Gnat.

The car drew close; a VW Jetta with an Auburn tag on the front. The driver was his old insurance agent. She passed with a wave that got a gun blast in response. The passenger-side rear window shattered, but the Jetta kept rolling. Gnat yelled like a soldier caught up in battle. He stood in the middle of the road and squeezed off another round. The rear windshield shattered. The Jetta swerved to the left and went off the bank at the bridge, landing with a metallic crunch and rising smoke.

"Roll Tide, Roll," Gnat laughed. "Ain't that right, pal?"

"Roll Tide." Sam would say anything because only two bullets were left in the chamber, and his odds of escape had improved.

"Better pick up the pace," Gnat said. "I don't want our game to have a crap ending."

He doubted that any ending would be crap for old Gnat. The drug addict would have his thrill no matter if he killed some random stranger driving by or put the bullet into the base of Sam's skull. The thrill was the kill—just like hunting—something Sam knew about. Little gave a man a rush like taking down a deer. He decided his hunting days were over, even if he survived the walk.

He and Gnat continued up the road, quicker now. The cemetery drew closer and closer. The big old tombstones came into clear view. *I got a chance. I'll run and hide. He'll shoot off a round, maybe two, and then I can take him.* Gnat walked on the pavement, and Sam walked on the grassy shoulder.

An old beast roared. Sam recognized the sound as it rumbled from behind them. He glanced back at a faded tan pickup truck rumbling over the bridge. It slowed as the driver looked at the wreck, and then sped back up. *He's seen us. He thinks we wrecked. Don't stop.*

"Looks like your luck gets better and better." Joy brimmed in Gnat's voice.

"Don't do it, Gnat. I know him. He's a good man; I work with him."

"Then what's his name?"

"Preacher Meeks. That's what we call him. He's a pastor at some little country church."

"He ought to be ready to meet his maker."

The truck pulled beside them. The window was down.

"You boys have a wreck?" Preacher Meeks asked.

"No, Preacher, we're fine just keep on going," Sam said.

"Shut up." Gnat pulled the pistol up and shot.

Sam watched blood erupt from the back of Preacher Meeks' head and splatter on the passenger-side window. The truck lurched and rolled across the road. Gnat and Sam stood back. The pickup bounced into the cemetery and knocked over one of the high, old tombstones.

"I got one bullet left, man. Don't try that again."

Sam nodded his agreement and gave up his plan to hide among the graves. A sick feeling welled up inside of him. The urge to vomit seemed overwhelming. For the first time since Gnat got the slip on him, Sam's mouth was moist, too moist. He felt like he'd choke on his spit. They went down a hill. At the base, before going around a small bend in the road, he bent over and expelled the excess saliva and some stomach contents into the high dead weeds.

"Not got the stomach for this?" Gnat asked. "Don't worry. Can't be much longer, I suppose."

Sam straightened up and wiped his mouth with his torn sleeve. They walked around the bend. Sam's house came into view. Even with the waves of nausea still washing over him, he plotted his run to the door. His wife wouldn't be home yet, so he didn't worry about that. Each footstep brought them nearer. Beams of yellow and orange fading sunlight illuminated it like something from a dream. His wife's car pulled out of the driveway and drove toward them. Sam's guts dropped, and vomit almost spewed forth again. He nearly broke out running, but something kept him from it. Fear cemented him in place. He didn't want to die. The car grew closer.

"It's your lucky day," Gnat sounded cold and aloof.

"Not really."

Gnat looked at him and nodded. Sam knew he understood his meaning. The car got closer. Gnat pulled back the hammer. It clicked. Fear gripped Sam, locking him in place. His wife and his boy were in range.

I don't want to die. His mind screamed. His arms twitched. *I can't live without them.*

"It's your choice," Gnat said. "I'm gonna bet you lose either way."

Sam decided. The gun went off, and Sam felt the fiery result of his decision deep in his gut. Five spent cases remained in the cylinder of the .38, and the tendrils of gun smoke rose into the air. The game ended. Sam lost.

Dry Places

A few pictures hung on the walls of Arnie's office. They accompanied sayings that every addict and recovering addict should know. The one behind his desk chair read: Let go and let God. Arnie held close to that saying more than any of the rest. In his course of hard drug abuse and recovery, he'd gotten to the point that the only choice he had was to do just that.

Not a single day passed that Arnie didn't sit behind his desk and think about the day that his life changed for the positive. After years of wandering around from place to place abusing everything a human could, he found himself lying in an alley in Birmingham, Alabama. A needle he'd used several times still stuck out of his arm. His breath left him, and he couldn't catch it. All the contents of his bowels and bladder emptied and soaked through the pants that he'd been wearing for at least two months. The pavement underneath him burned from the midday heat of July, but he was so cold it didn't do anything for him.

Arnie knew he was dying. That's when he let go and let God. Everything went black. At some point, days later, he woke up in St. Vincent's ICU—a new man.

Now as he sat at his desk, he looked over the appointment lines of his planner. He had an intake scheduled for this afternoon. The gentlemen's name was Horace. Arnie looked forward to the opportunity to help another human being kick the habit. After God saved him from death, he'd thrown all of himself into the work he'd been called to do—helping people with rehab. It consumed his whole life.

There came a knock at his door. Arnie stood and walked to it. When he opened it, a thin man, mostly skin and bones, stood propped against the wall. His cheeks sank in as did his eyes. Yellow skin stretched over the man's skeletal features. He looked like walking jaundice. Arnie had gotten to this guy just in time.

"Are you Horace?" he asked.

"That's me. I have an appointment."

"I've been expecting you. Come on in and sit down."

Arnie introduced himself and welcomed the man into his office. He patted the back of the old vinyl chair that clients sat in. The man dragged himself to it and sat. Arnie thought if he listened close enough he might hear the rattling of bones. The smell emanating from the man was something akin to a two-week-old corpse. Everything about him seemed unhealthy and necrotic.

"So how are you today?" Arnie walked around his desk and settled into his chair.

The man stared at him. From the deep recesses of his skull, his eyes seemed full of life and emotion. "How do you think I feel?"

"I don't know. That's why I asked, but if you've come to me for help, I'm going to guess not so good."

"On the nose." Horace touched his nose with a long boney finger. "You ought to go on *Jeopardy!*"

Arnie didn't care for sarcasm at any time—not from addicts and especially not from someone in Horace's condition. He had no right to behave like he was better than a healthy, recovering addict. Arnie jotted down the response on the questionnaire that was part of the admission process. The emotion in the man's eyes lingered. Arnie realized it was hate.

"Why are you so angry, Horace?"

"I'm not angry, Arnie. Why are you transferring your emotions onto me?"

"I'm not. You are being defensive, which is a sign of anger. Your eyes also speak volumes."

"So do yours."

"You chose to come for this intake. I didn't make you."

Horace's eyes brightened, and an eyebrow cocked upward. "Didn't you?"

Arnie decided that he was not going to accomplish anything by continuing this line of questioning. He turned back to his assessment. The words on the plaque above his head filled him up, and he took strength from them. The Serenity Prayer hung across the room from his desk. The words were printed in large, bold letters that made it easy to read.

God grant me the serenity to change the things I can, accept things I cannot change, and the wisdom to know the difference.

"Prayer is the last ditch effort of the hopeless," Horace said.

"What do you mean?"

"You were praying just then. Why are you hopeless? Am I an impossible case?"

"I was praying because that's what I do before all assessments." Arnie felt a knot in the pit of his stomach. It seemed that despite the fact that he looked half-dead, Horace was as perceptive as a healthy man.

"You can believe that lie if you want to." Horace smiled, his teeth little more than black rotten nubs right at the gum line.

Arnie tried not to look at him. Everything about this intake made him uncomfortable, and he was positive that the man was reveling in that. "What's your drug of choice?" he asked.

"What's yours?" Horace asked back.

"When I was an active addict, it was heroin."

The black nub teeth revealed themselves again. "How ironic. It's my drug of choice, too. I would marry it if I could."

"I understand that. I felt the same way. She was quite a mistress." He wrote heroin on the form. "It almost killed me."

"I know."

The knot in his stomach tightened. His mouth started to dry out. He wished he'd brought a cup of water with him to the interview. To go for one now could give the impression of disinterest and risk discouraging the man from seeking help. Arnie felt his salvation was balanced on how many addicts he could help, and he was determined not to fail at his calling.

"Why do you want to get off drugs?" Arnie asked.

"I don't"

"So why are you here?"

"Because of you."

Horace reached across the desk and grabbed Arnie's wrist. The addict's hand was hot and callused. The heat radiated up Arnie's arm, like when he used to push the first syringe of smack in the morning.

Arnie's memories rushed back to the first time he'd shot up. Sandra, a girl he'd met at a rave, took him into the bathroom. She pushed him up against the wall and started to work him over with her mouth. He couldn't resist her. It might have been her oral expertize but was more likely due to the Molly. He took her on the nasty, damp bathroom floor. The experience ended quickly. While he panted, propped against the wall, she reached in her purse and brought out her junky prep kit.

"Do you want to feel something better than any orgasm you've ever had?" she'd asked.

"Yeah."

They cooked a quick couple of CCs of smack and shot it up. The experience was like none other before—except for this one right now as the decrepit man held his arm. It was better than the first time he ever rode the horse.

Arnie came back to himself and jerked his arm away from Horace. His head swam, maybe from the memory, or the adrenaline pumping through his body.

"Please don't do that," he said.

"Sorry." The face full of black nub teeth smiled back at him.

"Do you have any medical problems?"

"Look at me. What do you think?"

Horace no longer smiled at him. His skin was still deep yellow, but the sunken cheeks seemed puffier. There was obviously something wrong with him, but Arnie had no idea what.

"I can tell you're not healthy, but do you have any diseases?"

"Hep C, genital herpes, hypertension, general malaise."

Arnie jotted down the diseases on the form. The letters were shaky and crooked. He tried to steady his hand, but the tremor continued. His hand hadn't shaken like that since he'd been riding the horse. Horace's sunken eyes studied Arnie's quivering hand.

"Looks like you got a nasty case of the shakes," he said. "Maybe you should pray again."

"For what? They'll go away. Sometimes I get shaky if my blood sugar drops." Arnie reached into the drawer of his desk. He took out a soft peppermint ball. "This will fix it."

He popped the candy into his mouth. The sweet sugar started to melt. The flavor of peppermint exploded in his mouth like nothing he'd ever tasted. He smelled it and was pretty sure he heard it sizzle on his tongue. All his senses turned on full. The light in his office almost blinded him. He remembered such an explosion of sensation the first few times he'd shot up heroin. His hand no longer trembled.

"You shouldn't lie," Horace said. "God doesn't like it."

"What do you know about God? So far all you've done is make light of my faith and my God."

The anger inside Arnie came out quick and fiery. He reached across and knocked the other man's arms off the desk.

"I am not making light of God, but I don't believe your faith," Horace said.

Arnie's hands trembled again, but this time with the rage building inside him. All the extrasensory activity ceased, but the built-up energy packed itself into the emotional rampage inside him.

"What do you know about faith? It's all I have. If it hadn't been for mine, I'd look like you, on death's door."

"You have your memories."

"My faith helps keep my memories at bay," Arnie said. "Those things can get me into trouble. They can get any addict into trouble. That's why you let go and let God."

"And he just takes care of everything?"

"You don't have faith in anything, do you?"

Horace shook his head. "No, I believe there is a God. I have faith that there is."

Arnie swallowed, and the brief time between that action and speaking again cleared his head. "That's a start. The first step we use here to gain recovery is to reach an understanding that there are greater things than ourselves."

"There are many things greater than me. I know that." Horace's voice softened. The junkie's lip quivered, and his eyes clouded with what must have been tears.

Arnie reached for a box of tissue and passed it to him, but Horace grabbed hold of the counselor's hand again. Arnie fought the urge to jerk away like he had before. This time the addict was reaching out to a former addict. This was the breakthrough moment.

"Let go and let God," Arnie said. "When you do that, the demon of addiction will leave you and go back to the hell where it came from."

Horace's grip moved up to Arnie's forearm. With a stiff tug, the junkie pulled the counselor to his feet. Arnie wanted to pull away but didn't. If Horace needed this kind of contact to give himself over to recovery and the Higher Power, then he would allow it, even though the stench of the man sickened him. Horace's hug crushed Arnie's arms to his sides, forcing him into a painful bent position.

"Tell me—what do you fill your time with so that you don't go back on junk?"

The breath from the words burrowed into Arnie's ear like warm water, dripping toward his brain. Everything changed. The junkie's words echoed through his skull as the world swirled in front of him.

Deep inside himself, Arnie searched for the answer. What had he filled his time with? Magnificent colors swirled around him as he saw himself falling down an impossible chasm. His mind snapped back inside his body. He ached all over, and his stomach roiled with spasms. The roof of his mouth felt like sandpaper as he brushed his tongue across it. Parched and overwhelmed by oppressive heat, Arnie opened his eyes just a slit.

Harsh white light filled his vision. He blinked. Sunlight beat down on him from high in a pale, blue summer sky. A rock dug into his back. He wanted to move and get up but couldn't. His limbs wouldn't cooperate. The sunlight burned his eyes. He tried to close his lids, but they too wouldn't obey him. Tightness ringed his arm. He knew that feeling—an elastic band like what a phlebotomist used when drawing blood. Without seeing it, Arnie knew that a needle and syringe stuck out of his arm. His bladder and bowels let go.

As he lay in his own filth, he relived the worst and best day of his life. Arnie felt his life slipping away from him in that Birmingham alley. He prayed to God. The prayer was to not let him die. He wanted to let go and let God. It was in the Bible, was it not? Why else would so many of those programs use it? No sooner had he said amen in his head than he felt his life quit seeping away. Before he slipped into unconsciousness, he caught a glimpse of a shadowy creature escape into the air. It looked down at him from a skull-like face made of what appeared to be smoke. It looked familiar.

"Are you okay?" Horace asked.

Arnie looked at him. Everything seemed unreal, dream-like, like what he'd just experienced was his reality. It couldn't be, though. He'd live out that episode two years ago.

What have I filled my time with since then? He mulled over what the junkie had said. The answer was that he had done nothing to fill his time. All he had been able to do was think about the times when he had stayed stoned. He'd told himself to focus on getting others clean, but the ugly truth was that he talked to them just to remember the thrill of use.

"Get out," Arnie said.

"What?"

"I can't help you."

"What do you mean? I thought this was your calling from God."

He looked at Horace. The junkie didn't look like someone pleading for help. He looked lean and ravenous. His eyes had verve in them.

"I thought it was. I was wrong," Arnie said. "Get out."

"But you've already helped me so much."

"How?"

"I've let go and let God," Horace said.

"That's bullshit. Somebody just made it up. It's not even in the Bible." Arnie's words tore into his throat as he said them.

He'd never had true faith. Now it was clear. All he'd believed in was the twelve-step philosophy and some pseudo-religious stuff. The blue book had been his Bible, and he'd been a horrible disciple. Heroin hadn't coursed through his veins in a long time, but the horse galloped through is memory several times every day.

"You are right about the Bible," Horace said. "Nowhere does it say that you should let go and let God—at least, not in those words."

Arnie watched Horace change from a solid figure into a smoky shadow of a man. The man's eyes caught and held Arnie's attention. They were the eyes he'd seen leave him in the alley two years prior.

"It does say that if you lose a demon you should fill your life with good things or the demon will return," Horace said, "and he'll return with friends."

"What are you talking about?"

The shadowy figure rose and moved toward him. Arnie tried to get away, but the demon slipped down his throat like heavy opiate-laced smoke. His whole body became warm just like it did with the drugs. All his thoughts slowed down, and his mind numbed. He called out in his head for God's help. Instead the urge to shoot up became overwhelming. He was in bad need of the junk, a craving worse than any other need he had ever experienced.

***

Arnie sat with his back against the cold bricks of an abandoned building. Through gauzy eyes, he observed the world. A dreamy smile covered his lips. Heroin coursed through his body, warming him like a thick blanket. Tiny dragons danced in front of him as three voices in his head discussed the Bible. One claimed to be God, but Arnie wasn't sure. The voice kept telling him to kill people like the mayor and Roy Rogers. The other claimed to be Little Orphan Annie and sang about hard-knock lives. And then there was the third.

"Nothing like coming home," the voice called Horace said. "Home, sweet home."

Twinkle Lights

The red and green lights on the small silver Christmas tree blur together as Brett opens his eyes. The glowing numbers of his alarm clock match the hue of the green Christmas lights. It's two in the morning, and someone has slammed his front door. It's his luck to be robbed on Christmas.

He climbs out of bed and fumbles for the baseball bat that he keeps beside his bed for such an emergency. The twinkle lights on the small tree sitting on his dresser shine enough light to walk across his bedroom without tripping over his discarded clothes or stubbing his toes on the corners of his furniture.

With the bat in grand-slam position, Brett creeps into the hallway. His own door creaks on its hinges as he opens it. Nothing stirs in the house. His family left to stay at his grandparents' overnight. He would join them when morning came, true morning, the kind that came with sunshine not just minutes past midnight, but he'd stayed at home after visiting with his girlfriend and her family. As he walks into the living room, only the electric candles in the window shed light. He walks to the door and jiggles the handle. It's locked. Even the deadbolt is set.

"Must have been dreaming," he says out loud.

Something scrapes across the front window. Brett jumps, almost breaking the glass with his bat. He pushes back the curtain and peeps outside. Something horrible stares back in at him, his own sleep-weary face crowned with his out-of-control bed hair. The reflection scares him.

The curtain falls back into place. He feels five-years-old, afraid of being in the house alone. This is what he wanted, though. He remembers ranting in his dorm room about how Christmas used to have ghost stories and real frights.

"Well, Ebenezer, you've lucked up. This is the visit from Jacob Marley that you wanted," he says aloud. "A good old-fashion Christmas spook tale."

He starts back to his bedroom, letting the bat drag behind. A loud banging comes from the laundry room at the back of the house where the garage door is. It is the sound of that heavy metal door slamming. Brett pulls the bat back up to attack mode and heads down the hallway past his room and into the laundry room. He flips on the light to dispel the gloom and to surprise whoever slammed the door.

Only the washer-dryer combo and a few ghosts of laundry days past greet him when the light flickers on. The door is closed, the security chain in place. Something moves outside the small casement window. Brett peeps out but sees only his own reflection. He begins to think he might be dreaming. Then his bedroom door slams.

Brett runs back to his room. The door is closed, although it stood open when he'd walked past it just a few moments before. He opens it and rushes in to find no one. His window curtains rustle. He moves them aside and finds two glowing red eyes staring at him. His own reflection reveals his horror as another pair of glowing green eyes approaches him from behind.

He turns around as an impish creature lurches toward him with drool dripping from its mouth. Glass shatters as another imp jumps through the window. It looks the same as the one already in the room except for possessing glowing red eyes.

Brett swings his bat at the green-eyed imp. It ducks, and the bat sails over its head. He turns around and takes another swing at the thing from the window. It grabs the bat with its clawed hand. Brett's shoulder twists out of place as the window imp wrenches it from his hand. The imp snaps the thick wood. Two pieces of bat thud to the floor. Brett backs against his bed to shrink away from the things. He wills himself to wake from the nightmare.

Neither of the things says a word as they advance on him. Both pounce and knock him to the bed. They suck the air like drinking from a straw. Brett feels his life-force escape his body until he sees nothing but four glowing eyes, two red and two green like twinkle lights blinking out a message of Christmas cheer. He shuts off his mind with the final memory that all he wanted for Christmas is a really good scare. Isn't he lucky.

New Orleans' Best Beignets

Maurice Devereaux needed a job, and L'Enfant Bakery on Jackson Street was hiring. According to some of his sources, Denis L'Enfant would hire anyone as long as they were clean: both bathed and drug-free. Maurice could claim both, although he'd only been drug-free for a year.

The bakery looked nice. It sat between two microbreweries that popped up after Katrina. Before that, Maurice seemed to remember that an Irish pub took up one of the spaces. The other had been a cheap souvenir joint that sold Mardi Gras beads all year. L'Enfant Bakery had always been there. Before the storm, it was run down; the lettering on the windows had chipped off, and few people ate there. They called it "L'Infection Bakery." Even Maurice refused to eat there at his worst, which he thought was saying something, because he'd eaten out of the dumpsters at the Superdome and drank Hurricanes tourists abandoned on the street, even those with cigarette butts in them.

Now he, a cleaned-up man, stood outside the cleaned-up bakery. The words on the windows stared in festive New Orleans colors. The decorative wrought iron lampposts out front were glossy black. All the neon in the signs glowed fresh. *Voted New Orleans' Best Beignets* was scrolled in gold letters across both windows.

Maurice caught his reflection. He looked darker than before he'd been shipped off to Angola. Some smart-alecky coon-ass might even tell him he looked like one of the freshly painted lampposts. In the old days, he'd have fought over that. But just like his city, he'd changed through time and hardship. He hoped he was better as he stepped into the cool, sugar-scented air of the bakery. Bells jingled as he walked in. The dining area was bereft of customers, but a stout man dressed in white stood behind the counter.

"Can I help you?" the man asked.

"I came because I heard that y'all might be hiring," Maurice said, twisting his hands in front of his chest.

"I think I heard Mr. L'Enfant say something about that. He's in the back, at the soup kitchen. I'll step back there and get him."

"Y'all serve soup here too?"

"Naw, after the storm, when he got his huge insurance check, Mr. L'Enfant said he wanted to give something back. So he bought the store that opened up from our back onto the next street and turned it into a soup kitchen for the homeless." The man wiped his hands on his apron. "I'll go get him. Sit tight."

Maurice nodded and sat at a table near the door. Maybe his sources had been right. If Mr. L'Enfant ran a soup kitchen, he'd probably hire a convicted felon too. As far as Maurice knew, the man he'd just talked to might have gotten out of Angola yesterday, just like him.

A red checked tablecloth covered the table where he sat. Powder sugar formed small hills all over the plastic cloth. Maurice remembered places—darker places—with small piles of white powder on tables. Most of the time he'd either sold the stuff on display or been stocking his supply-line. He never cared much for blow, and, as Whitney Houston had put it, "crack is whack." Maurice only smoked weed, but had been clean since arriving at Angola. He'd been sent up on dealing, plea-bargained down from trafficking. As much as the sirens of his old life called to him, a second chance lay before him, and he wanted to give life his best shot, even if it meant frying beignets for the tourists and staying free of the reefer.

"Sure hope I ain't been keeping you too long."

Maurice looked up from the sugar on the table and snapped back from his daydream. A plump man wearing a white apron over blue striped seersucker pants and a light blue shirt walked toward him from the counter. A broad white smile cut through his deep dark skin.

"Mr. L'Enfant?" Maurice asked, standing and extending his hand.

"The one and only. At least in this store."

The handshake was one good pump with a tight grip. L'Enfant's hands were hard as rocks. Maurice never imagined a pastry chef having such hard hands. The man's smile beamed at him and sincerity bloomed from it. Maurice had seen millions of insincere smiles in his time, and it was clear that L'Enfant sold his over-the-top grin as well as he did his beignets.

L'Enfant motioned for them to sit at the table. He brushed the sugar from the tablecloth with a quick sweep of his hand. "Beau tells me you're looking for a job."

"Yessir."

"As you can see, I need some help around here. I can't even keep the tables clean."

"I thought maybe you were having a dry spell, seeing as how no one's here," Maurice said.

L'Enfant's laughter echoed around the empty bakery like thunder rolling over the bayou. "Everybody knows that I don't serve beignets at this time of the day. I devote this hour to my soup kitchen out back." He eyed Maurice. "Just get out of the joint?"

Maurice looked down at the pattern on the table cloth. The large red checks were in reality a series of smaller pink and red checks. "Yessir."

"Ain't no reason to be embarrassed around me, son. Everybody gets in a little trouble now and then. I hire all sorts—actually I like hiring ex-cons. Gives 'em the chance to start over."

"I heard you hire a lot of us." Maurice looked into L'Enfant's sparkling, dark brown eyes. "I heard you're a good man."

"Son, ain't got nothing to do with being good; got everything to do with being blessed. Katrina gave me a chance to start over and better myself. I took it. Now I offer the same to others, but without the trauma of that storm."

The man from earlier poked his head back into the bakery. "Mr. L'Enfant, I need you back here."

L'Enfant stood and held his hand back out to Maurice. "Congratulations, Mr....?"

"Devereaux. Maurice Devereaux."

"Mr. Devereaux, you've got a job cooking beignets for me on the graveyard shift. Show up tonight 'round midnight. I'll wait around and help get you started."

They shook, and L'Enfant hurried back to the soup kitchen. Maurice wanted to cheer. He'd not had a straight job since he worked at McDonald's as a teenager. The money wouldn't be anything like he made dealing, but the benefit of staying out of Angola was enough. He looked at his watch; he'd need some sleep before tonight. Maurice rushed out of the bakery, the bell on the door clattering loudly.

***

Maurice walked into L'Enfant's Bakery through the front door. He couldn't hear the jangle of the door over the crowd of customers. Glasses and coffee mugs clinked as they hit the tables. A baby squealed. The whole dining room buzzed with chatter, all the tourists enjoying a late night pastries. Plates of powdered sugar-laden beignets covered nearly every table. A line that stopped short of the door ran to the check-out register.

The door to the kitchen burst open, and L'Enfant hustled out a tray of what looked like ordinary donuts. Maurice didn't figure they sold much more than beignets. L'Enfant looked up as he placed the tray in the glass display counter.

"Maurice," he said. "Come on back."

Maurice broke between two people in line and walked behind the counter. L'Enfant shook his hand again with his signature firm, single pump, his thick palm sticky with donut glaze. They walked back to the kitchen. The smell of the baking pastries hit Maurice in the face like a soft punch. He didn't mind because it meant honest work, although it was a bit overwhelming for his personal taste.

"The first thing is this," L'Enfant grabbed an apron from a hook and slung it at Maurice. "I don't care too much about what you wear to work as long as you wear an apron and hair net." He looked at Maurice's head. "I guess you don't need one."

"I keep it slick. It's cooler this way." Maurice rubbed his shaved head before pulling the apron's top loop over it. He crossed the side strings behind him then bow-tied the front. "So what am I doing?"

L'Enfant led him to a large industrial mixer, then turned it on. It whirled with a loud mechanical noise. "You make sure the batter is nice and mixed." The mixer stopped, and L'Enfant dipped a long spoon into the bowl. "If this comes up without any dry mix on it, you're set. Easy enough."

Maurice nodded. "I think I can handle that. I worked in the kitchen some at Angola. We never had anything nice as this, though."

"All mixers pretty much work the same. What were you in Angola for?"

"Stupidity."

L'Enfant roared a laugh and slapped Maurice on the back with the same force as he shook hands. "Everybody ends up in there for that or being wrongfully accused. What kind of stupidity?"

Maurice didn't know if it was legal for L'Enfant to ask him that, but the baker had hired him with no other questions. "Dealing. Big-time dealing."

"All right. I've had a couple of big-time dealers. I want to introduce you to your supervisor." L'Enfant pointed at a small, wiry man sitting at a desk. "That's Bruce."

Bruce looked up with a blank expression and then back down at the *Times-Picayune*.

"Hey."

"Bruce isn't much for conversation. If you have any problems, bring them to him." L'Enfant led Maurice away and whispered, "He's not here as a dealer. He got out early for good behavior after murder one was brought down to manslaughter."

"How 'bout breaks or lunch?" Maurice asked.

"Bruce will tell you when to go. By the way, here it's all you can eat, so take advantage of it. We make the best beignets in New Orleans, maybe the world."

Maurice nodded and went back to the mixer. He switched it on and let it whirl. A few minutes later, he put the spoon into the batter to check the mixture, then passed the bowl down the line. Another bowl of ingredients awaited him. Before he realized it, he'd fallen into a pattern, and time passed quickly.

"Break time," Bruce called out. His voice was heavy like lead and thick with the bayou. "Make sure to eat some of the beignets."

Maurice looked over his shoulder. "I'm okay. I don't like them that well."

"Understand, on my shift you have to eat beignets." Bruce grabbed his arm with vise-like force.

Spikes of pain shot up his arm. He turned enough to see the small man's face; a smirk stretched his lips. Bruce meant business, and Maurice got the hint.

"I think I'm craving a beignet," Maurice said.

The pressure on his arm went away. "We understand each other, then," Bruce said. "I make sure Mr. L'Enfant has a certain amount of beignets eaten each night. It's how I stay the manager. Get it?" Maurice rubbed his arm. "Yeah, got it."

Bruce handed Maurice a plate full of pastries. "Take it to the back in the soup kitchen's dining room. That's where we take all our breaks."

Maurice took the plate and walked through the door marked *Soup Kitchen*. He arrived in a large empty room full of long tables. The air felt stale and smelled of the homeless. He knew the smell well. A short time before getting shipped to Angola he'd spent some time living on the streets himself. L'Enfant was a good man to spend so much time and effort helping the down and out. Maybe Maurice would volunteer some of his free time to work the kitchen.

He sat at the first table and bit into one of the beignets. Why didn't he just throw them away instead of eating them? But that question quickly vanished from his mind when he realized how amazing they tasted. He shoved in another. If all the beignets he'd eaten tasted like these, he would've eaten them twenty-four/seven. He shoved another in before swallowing. Then another. And another. Soon he needed something to drink.

A scan of the room came up empty. And he noticed the place didn't look right. The area where the sink and counter should have been was blocked by a metal gate that looked like a garage door. Everything seemed clean, despite the smell. It looked more like a coffee house or an upscale café than any soup kitchen he'd seen while living on the streets. Maybe that was L'Enfant's idea. The homeless didn't enjoy their plight, and a standard soup kitchen did nothing but remind them of who they were.

The door to the kitchen burst open, and Bruce hustled in. The noise of the door hitting the wall brought Maurice's focus back. He looked at Bruce. The ex-murderer looked put out, flexing his hand in and out of a fist.

"What are you doing?" Bruce asked.

"I'm on break. You forced me in here and made me eat these beignets."

"That was forty-five minutes ago. Get back in here, we're swamped."

Maurice wiped his mouth on his apron and hurried back into the kitchen. True to Bruce's words, everyone seemed to move faster and work harder. A red-faced kid huffed as he moved a bowl from the mixer Maurice worked on. The boy's shirt under his apron was too tight, and a bit of his white belly hung from it.

"Let me help you with that," Maurice said, taking the bowl. "You look like you're about to pass out."

"I think I might be," the boy said. "I don't know when I got so out of shape. When I got out of juvie at the beginning of the summer, I could run two miles and barely be puffin'. Now I can't walk from one end of the kitchen to the other without a break."

It was hard to believe the pudgy kid could do anything without getting winded, but Maurice noticed that the boy's arms had ropy muscles in them like one accustomed to the gym. The weight around the boy's gut seemed out of place. No waddle hung from his chin like others with pronounced bellies.

"Simons," Bruce barked. "Break time. Get your plate of beignets and get to it."

The boy rubbed his hands on his apron and patted Maurice on the shoulder. Then Simons grabbed a plate piled with beignets and disappeared into the soup kitchen's dining room. Maurice kept staring at the door.

"Get that bowl over here," Bruce yelled.

Maurice shook off his thoughts and scurried across the kitchen with the bowl of batter. He passed it off to the next cook and headed back to his mixer. Bruce followed and stood behind him as Maurice started the paddles whirling in the bowl. The older man's breath reeked of coffee and cigarettes.

"Do you have to stand behind me like that?" Maurice asked not looking back.

"I'm your supervisor. I'm supervising."

"Am I doing an okay job?"

Bruce grabbed him by the upper arm. "Mr. L'Enfant doesn't like his workers getting buddy-buddy. Remember that. He hires a bunch of cons like us and doesn't need us planning how to knock the joint over or sell dope out of his soup kitchen."

"I promise those days are done for me. I was just talking to Simons, trying to be friendly and such."

"Ain't no need to be 'friendly and such' with folks like Simons. Even by our standards he's trouble. Went up for rape, you see?"

Maurice knew that a hard con like Bruce didn't have time for rapists. He didn't either, but the kid looked so innocent. It was probably statutory. *Pity for a young guy to get that on his record.* "How long has he been here?"

"A few weeks," Bruce said, "but don't get too into that. You got work to do so get to it."

The supervisor let go of his arm and walked back to his desk and *Times-Picayune*. Maurice stopped the spinning paddles and tested the batter with his spoon. No dry flour. He moved the bowl down the line. As he walked past the soup kitchen's door, he peered in at the teenager gorging on beignets. If Simons had only been with the bakery a few weeks, he must have really put the pastries away. Maurice decided that he'd start throwing his out to keep from ending up with a saggy gut.

***

Maurice walked into the kitchen. Bruce sat at his desk reading his *Times-Picayune* as usual. L'Enfant stood by the mixing bowl area, a broad smile on his face.

"Maurice," L'Enfant said. "Guess what?"

"I don't know."

"You're getting a promotion and small raise."

"Really, to what?"

"It seems that Mr. Simons won't be coming back to us. Apparently, he's blown town."

Maurice's stomach sank. Simons had been his only friend in the kitchen. They talked a lot. Simons just got a new girlfriend who was of legal age. He was happy. Maurice couldn't imagine why he would blow town.

"Did he run off with his new girlfriend?" Maurice asked.

"Probably ran from the law," Bruce said, now standing beside Maurice. "Kid was stupid, started back into his old ways soon as he got out."

Maurice didn't like the coldness in his supervisor's voice. It seemed far too malicious. He also didn't understand how Simons could have gone back to his "old ways" since it had been statutory rape with his girlfriend. True, plenty who tried going straight eventually went back to their crimes. But Simons was a different breed.

"So get to work," L'Enfant said. He poked Maurice's belly, a belly that had started to grow pudgy. "Been hitting the beignets?"

Maurice felt his face flush a little. Although he'd tried to resist them, the beignets were irresistible. He dreamed about them and woke up wet and sticky.

L'Enfant left after patting Maurice on his back. Bruce guided him to his new position as shaper.

Maurice started rolling out the batter and putting the small balls on baking sheets. The stuff seemed stickier than it should. Years ago, he'd helped his grandmother make beignets for Christmas. They never seemed this sticky, but home cooking was not the same as industrial cooking. The ingredients had to be different.

The smell of the frying confections wafted toward Maurice. His mouth watered, and he felt aroused. Somehow the beignets tapped into his sexual instincts, as well as his hunger. He was glad for the apron to hide his arousal.

"Boss," one of the workers yelled across the kitchen. "We's running low on the shortening."

Bruce folded his paper and laid it on his desk. "We just got a new shipment in. Isn't it over there?"

"Nassir, it ain't."

"I'll go get it."

Bruce disappeared into the soup kitchen. Maurice never noticed a storage locker in that area. He rolled the dough and put it out on the sheets. A few minutes later, Bruce rolled a barrel in on a set of dollies. It was black with no writing on it. The top was off, and he could see into it.

The shortening inside appeared too yellow. He'd never seen shortening that wasn't snow white.

"What is that?" he asked Bruce.

"Shortening."

"I've never seen shortening like that."

Bruce glared at him, cold and hard. "It's special shortening. It's what makes Mr. L'Enfant's beignets so good."

When his break came, Maurice hadn't even realized it. Time passed like a shot while he thought about his missing friend. Bruce pushed him away from the pans and handed him his plate of beignets. His trousers tightened when his thumb brushed one of the pastries, and he hurried into the soup kitchen.

The first bite made him groan. The sugar touched his tongue with an explosion of flavor. The next bite sent him into a full orgasm. The pastries seduced him. Each lounged on the plate like a wanton lover. He satisfied them all, and they he. By the time only powdered sugar remained on the plate, Maurice dripped with sweat. He'd climaxed at least twice. No sex had caused him that much pleasure in that quick of succession. He waited for his hands to quit shaking and his legs to finish wobbling before he went back to work.

The kitchen bustled when he stepped back into its sultry heat. Everything seemed to vibrate with energy. He felt like he'd taken a couple hits of X. The world glowed and shimmered. Even Bruce looked softer.

"What's your problem?" Bruce asked.

Maurice grinned. "Nothing's wrong. Everything's right."

Bruce clenched him around the arm. "Get back to work and wipe that stupid grin off your face."

Maurice tried, but it came right back. He felt the small muscles at the edge of his lips stretch and pull. "Sorry, I can't."

Bruce pinched the fat on Maurice's belly and twisted. Maurice quit smiling.

"That did it," Bruce said. "Getting a bit fatty, aren't you?"

Maurice wanted to curse his boss, but anger faded fast and his grin returned. He felt too good to let some screw like Bruce bring him down. Whatever had him so high, he needed it in pill form; he could make a million pushing the stuff.

"Whatever."

Bruce's expression didn't change. "I've got another shipment of shortening arriving first thing in the morning. I need you to stay behind and help me."

"Whatever."

***

Maurice followed Bruce into a stairwell behind the soup kitchen. It wound down to the storeroom below the bakery. Everything smelled like burnt bacon, and he almost wretched. Whatever took him up so high last night was now killing him, and he wondered if Bruce, to get him fired, had laced some of the beignets, but he'd sampled about every drug out there. None of them had made him feel like that, not Molly, heroin or crack.

"So they're delivering down here? I don't see a door to the street," Maurice said as they walked into a large empty storage area.

"This is where the shortening arrives," Bruce said.

A chair sat in the middle of the floor. A plastic drop cloth lay across the floor and under the chair. A series of old oil drums sat a few feet from the chair. Hoses ran to them from a machine on the far wall. It hummed, and the instruments glowed in the gloom.

"Sit," Bruce said. "It's going to be a few minutes before it gets here, and you've been on your feet all night."

"I'm good," he said, but he wasn't. He couldn't seem to shake a feeling of vertigo. Everything swirled around him, and Bruce seemed weirder than usual.

"Nonsense. Mr. L'Enfant wants you taking care of yourself. Sit."

The world spun. Maurice wobbled to the chair and sat. He figured it was better to give in than fall. Bruce was up to something behind him, but Maurice didn't move lest he be overtaken by the spinning world again.

"Hello, Maurice."

He looked up to see Mr. L'Enfant smiling at him.

"Good morning."

"Glad to see you looking so well." He brought out a plastic cup from behind his back. "Don't mind taking a pee test for me, do you?"

"What?"

"I've had a tip that you've gone back to your old ways, Maurice. Ex-cons are fine employees. Current cons aren't."

"I'll pee in your cup, but I've done nothing wrong."

L'Enfant handed him the cup. "Prove it."

Maurice took the cup and stood. "Where's the bathroom?"

"Right here."

He closed his eyes, unzipped his fly, and pissed in the cup. When he felt the warmth of urine touch his penis, he stopped. Opening his eyes, he handed the cup back to Mr. L'Enfant.

"There."

L'Enfant took a plastic stick from his pocket and stirred it in the urine. A short moment later, he studied the dripping stick and shook his head.

"Positive."

"I've not done anything," Maurice protested.

"You're fired."

"I was set up. Was it Bruce? He's been after me. I've even been thinking about it. I think he may have something to do with Simons being gone."

L'Enfant's smile grew wider. "I know that."

Maurice turned and saw Bruce approaching him with an old fire ax. He tried to move away, but the world swirled again. The chair caught him when he fell. "Simons is still around," L'Enfant said. "He's probably under your fingernails. We started using him last night."

"The shortening."

"After Katrina, it got hard to find shortening, but we were heavy on the homeless and dead. I rendered some hobo fat one day and used it for my beignets. They were magnificent. By the looks of you, I think you'll make a good batch," L'Enfant said. "I make the special ones for my employees. A little hoodoo makes them extra tasty and extra fattening. It also takes the fight out of the tough ones, like you."

"But why us?"

"Less criminals in the world the better," L'Enfant said. "Plus success don't come cheap. A body has to almost sell his soul to get to my level. Problem is I like my soul. The souls of hoods, like yourself and Simons, are hell-bound already. Just helping y'all along."

"I can do things," Maurice said with a clarity that surprised him.

"I don't need the kind of services you learned to perform in the joint," L'Enfant said, waving his hand to Bruce.

The henchman stepped up drawing the ax back ready to deliver the blow. Maurice put his hands up and fell to his knees.

"That ain't what I'm offering. I can make a clean kill, and bring in twice as many workers. I know how to talk to hoods," Maurice said.

L'Enfant studied him. Maurice felt fat drops of sweat run down his face. His boss stared into his eyes. They pierced deep inside of him. Maurice willed L'Enfant to believe him. Never had he been so desperate to live. If they hadn't drugged him with whatever they used, he could have fought off both of them. The chemicals running through his system left him drained and a little aroused.

L'Enfant took the ax from Bruce. He drew it over his head and brought it down quickly, stopping a breath from Maurice's skull. L'Enfant smiled like he had the day they met.

"Prove it," he nodded toward Bruce.

Maurice jumped to his feet with a newfound fervor. He gripped the ax. It felt good in his hand as if it had been part of his arm since birth. He would show L'Enfant what he was worth.

***

Jack read the article on L'Enfant's Bakery in the *Times-Picayune*. He was set to get out of Angola the next day and planned on heading back to New Orleans. Mr. Devereaux, the skills teacher in the pen, told him about the bakery. He read up on it because they hired cons who were clean. It sounded like a great place to work, and Jack was excited.

The article ended with the owner, Mr. L'Enfant, talking about how every employee took part in making the best beignets in New Orleans.

There's a little bit of our cooks in each one.

Jack needed to take pride in something. He looked forward to getting that job.

The Silver Needle

The ad strikes me as an oddity in my little hometown newspaper as I re-read it standing in line. The half-page two-color ad announces an old-time minstrel show being held at the Jaycee's fairground. A drawing of a banjo sits in the middle of the words. The orange color looks like the shade used on Halloween decorations. The selling point for me is the bold lettering: ONE NIGHT ONLY.

A poster of the same ad hangs on an old piece of paneling leaned against the chain-link fence that separates the grass-speckled parking lot from the dusty fairway of the fairground. The air smells of roasting peanuts, popcorn and other carnival foods. The music playing over the old gray loudspeaker sticking up from the side of the ticket booth is hard to hear over the roars and chants of protesters held at bay by sawhorses and police officers.

"Bigot!" One woman with a high-pitched voice yells at me as I advance up the line to the ticket booth.

"Nazi hate mongers!" Another woman in the crowd hollers.

I'm sure she's not talking to me because I've dressed down for the night. I left all the black SS clothes at home. I don't always wear them, and something about tonight told me to be different. The men behind me didn't have the same idea. Each wears his khaki Dickies work shirt with a hand-stitched red armband with an embroidered swastika on it. After I get my ticket, I plan to ask them where they bought them.

"God hates the haters," a black voice sings as I step up to the ticket booth.

"God hates jigaboos," the man behind me yells back. "God hates fags, spicks, chinks, Jews, and all those that love them."

The crowd hisses and screams louder. I feel them surge forward against the barriers as I pay my money and get my small green ticket. I walk into the fence as a police officer on a bullhorn warns the crowd to get back or they will be dispersed.

"Serves them damn right," the ticket taker in blackface with white grease paint around his lips says. "No reason for those brainwashed Jew lovers to be protesting. This isn't anything but a good clean show."

"Amen," I answer back. "I've got my right to free speech too."

"And defend it to the end against those Zionists who want the whole world run by kikes." He pats me on the shoulder as he hands me half my ticket back. "Enjoy the show. You'll never see another one like it."

I know he spoke the truth. The people in this town would never let another show like this come through again. It surprises me that I'm standing at the opening of the large Halloween orange and black tent. The smell of concessions floats out and waves me inside.

The lights inside the tent blind me. After a few minutes my eyes adjust, leaving only a few green blobs floating around in my vision. The risers aren't too high so I sit in the back next to the door. I don't trust the protesters outside. They always say they are about peace and love, but they aren't above throwing a brick or firebomb into a place like this. They're no better than those towel-head, camel jockeys that blew up the Trade Center. I hate them. All of them.

A tall man wearing a red and white striped tuxedo with tails walks out from the side of the tent. He holds an old-fashioned square microphone that hangs by a black wire from the roof. Thick black greasepaint covers his face except for a wide circle of pink around his lips. A curly black wig sticks out from under his tall red and white striped top hat.

"Ladies and gents," he uses a thick accent like old black men. "We's know that folks still coming in, but it's time for our show to gets started. So as the rest of y'all stream to yo seats. I's going to tell you a few things."

A smattering of clapping echoes through the tent mixing with some faint chuckling. I look around to the tent flap. A steady stream of men and women enter. Several wear khaki, white-power outfits, but some wear normal clothes.

"Again, ladies and gents, I be Uncle Herschel and this is my traveling minstrel show. We's here to entertain you and learns y'all a few good lessons 'bout all those thick-lipped, kinky headed darkies."

I clap as everyone in the whole tent burst into loud hoots and hollers.

"We's ready to start, Uncle Herschel," a black-faced actor yells from the flap. He jerks it closed, and the lights along the rim of the tent dim, leaving only the spots on the floor where the performance will be.

Butterflies flitter in my stomach as I wait for the show to start. They always dance and flutter when I'm about to see a concert or anything of the sort. Nothing I've seen so far would compare to this. The danger of getting mobbed at the end drives the butterflies into a frenzy. I hold my breath as I hear the first strums of a banjo and clank of a tambourine.

"Speakin' of the darkies, how about this old tune..." Uncle Herschel takes off his tall hat and holds it against his heart. He then warbles out a fast version of "Old Folks at Home." The microphone causes an echo effect when he sings about seeing all the darkies. My skin bursts into goose pimples as I clap and stomp my feet with all the others sitting on my riser.

The song ends, and Uncle Herschel walks off the stage. The banjo player picks another tune that no one sings. While he is playing, stagehands set up a scene that looks like the old South. The twang of the last banjo chord floats into the air while the crowd rouses a bunch of long whistles. I'm not a big fan of banjo picking, so I don't do much clapping or carrying on, and that's why I notice the exit flap.

At first, I don't believe my eyes. All the bright spotlights in the tent must be making my eyes play tricks on me, because I think I see a large needle sewing in and out of the thick canvas. The silver needle glitters in the light, and no hand pulls it back through. It sews on its own. As the next act starts, I register that twenty or more black-face mammies with red kerchiefs on their heads come out banging on tambourines and kicking their legs up. I turn my attention back to the phantom needle. The mammies sing about waiting for the *Robert E. Lee*. When the great general is mentioned, the crowd goes wild. Several men in front of me yell happy curses and chants of white power. I probably would join in if I hadn't caught sight of that damned needle.

Finally the needle sews down so low, I can't see it anymore. Nobody seems to notice it. I look for a way out. Those crazies protesting outside are going to try something, I know it. I'm going to get burned up in this tent with all these people. I don't want my mother finding out I died watching a black-face show with a bunch of racists. She would die of a heart attack if she ever knew my secret. I straighten up to see where the needle is, but it's gone. The whole flap is sewn shut with a row of neat stitches.

A flush of panic washes over me. My face feels hot, and beads of sweat form at the top of my forehead. I turn back around to the show. The dancing mammies end with a big circle dance of fluttering red skirts and clanging tambourines. The crowd goes nuts, clapping and stomping their feet. I join in not realizing what I'm doing. How long have I been sitting here? It seems like forever. That needle took half an hour to sew the flap shut, or it seemed that long. I look at my watch. It reads 8:30. It has to be wrong. I've only been sitting a little over thirty minutes. The air feels too hot for that amount of time that passed. It should take a mass of people this size twice as long to produce this much body heat.

"Ladies and gentlemen, I hopes you enjoyed waiting on the R. E. Lee. But now we's goin' break from the singing for just a minute. Enjoys our little sketch." Uncle Herschel's voice brought my focus back to the show.

An actress walked out in a large hoop dress like they wore during the Civil War. She fans herself with a feather fan and twirls a parasol. She hums a tune not meant to be identified. A Yankee soldier in blackface slinks onto the stage. He carries his musket in front of him like he's going to advance in a bayonet charge.

"Womans, I's been in this man's army a longs time, and I need some sugar," the soldier says.

"On my honor, sir, you are a Negro and a Yankee, and I will not be sullied by you," the belle answers

"Then I's takes it like Sherman took Atlanta."

The crowd hisses. I do too. It amazes me how I get caught up in the moment when everyone else is carrying on. The Yankee soldier grabs the belle. She screams, and he starts to make very theatrical kisses at her.

"Will no one save a belle from the rape of the Yankee Negro?"

A loud crack rings out like a firecracker exploding. I flinch, imaging the place bursting into flames with a misguided firework. A Confederate gray coat storms in from the other side of the stage. His saber flashes in the light. He waves it around making sure everyone sees it. The Yankee soldier backs off with an overacted reaction. His eyes grow large. He throws his hands up in surrender, dropping his musket.

"Die, you rapin' Yankee scum."

The Confederate sword pierces the empty space between the Yankee's arm and body. It is the death of children playing in the yard. I used to do the same thing playing pirates with my neighbor.

"I is smitten," the Yankee soldier says, lying down on the dirt.

The belle runs into the Confederate's arms and hugs him. She says something like my hero, but nothing is heard over the roars of the crowd. Cheers and loud whistles bound around the tent.

"Serves that coon right," someone below me yells.

Something's not right. The temperature keeps rising, and I start to think that firecracker caught something on fire after all. I fan myself with my hand as sweat rolls down my face and back. The Confederate and belle bow to the crowd. The Yankee stands and takes his bow too. Uncle Herschel steps back into the spotlight. Banjos, lots of them, strum to life, and tambourines jangle.

"Oh, I wish I was in the land of cotton. Old times there are not forgotten; look away, look away, look away, Dixieland."

Herschel sings the song fast, much faster than it should be, but the crowd stands and sings with him. The men in hats pull them off and hold them over their hearts. A few salute as the battle flag lowers from the ceiling. I stand but mostly to cool off. It feels like a mid-August day. Surely, my watch is broken, and the show nears its end. Then the twenty dancing, tambourine-shaking mammies come out singing "Dixie." They sing the first verse while Uncle Herschel starts the next. The crowd follows with Herschel. Now a dozen banjo pickers walk out followed by twenty more mammies.

The Confederate soldier unsheathes his sword. The Yankee does the same. A look of mischief crosses their faces. My mind registers this for a moment. The next thing I see sends the blood rushing through my veins.

The Confederate's sword glints in the lights as it slices through the air. A spray of red glitters in the same light. From the front row, a bald man's head tumbles through the air. Beside it, a woman with red hair screams as the Yankee's sword splits her skull open. More blood fountains into the air. The two soldiers push over the dead man and woman and move up the risers. The swords slice through air and the audience. Glints of sliver flash, and sprays of red splash. The singing becomes manic. I can no longer make out the words. The song becomes buzzing. It rises so loudly it drowns out the screams of terror as the two soldiers reap through the crowd.

When the mammies advance, I hurry to the edge of the risers ready to jump over the side. They are no longer in blackface, their faces ghostly, like skulls. They fan their tambourines at the crowd. Heads fall to the ground in twos and threes. The razor-sharp tumbrels splatter blood from the victims in a fine mist. The tent fills with a fog of dust and blood. I taste the coppery flavor and swallow down vomit. The soldiers are three seats from me. Their mouths draw back in a sinister grin, full of teeth and malevolence. The crowd stomps their feet and sings along. They are hypnotized, unaware of the carnage until it's too late.

I scramble over the metal railing on the riser and throw myself off. The ground comes up hard. My ankles roll beneath me, and a sharp pain streaks up my leg. Dark red blood puddles on the hard dirt floor. Uncle Herschel sings "Dixie" as if nothing is happening. I can hear him again, not the buzzing. The crowd screams and hollers its approval. Looking over my shoulder, I see more heads without bodies. A mammie swipes her tambourine at a skinhead with a swastika tattoo. His head comes free and flips through the air. She takes another swipe at it. The head lands beside me. Only one wide eye stares at me. The other is gone, cut out by the mammie. I drag myself to the flap and try to lift it from the ground. It won't budge.

I look up as the last of the soldiers reach the highest riser. Blood drips from the wooden plank seats. I lie in a mixture of bodily fluids. The smell permeates to my soul. Puke bursts from my lips unbidden. I press myself against the tent flap. The music stops. The last jangle of the tambourines fades away.

"Well looky heres, we got one left," Uncle Herschel walks up the empty aisle. "He must have seen the needle."

The others laugh as he walks closer. From behind his back, he pulls out a black-handled dagger. As he nears, I recognize it as one the SS used. I have a replica of it at home in my underwear drawer next to a few old copies of *Screw*.

"I didn't see anything," I say, holding my piss that begs to be let free. "If you let me go, I'll never tell a soul."

Uncle Hershel lords over me. His teeth shine whiter than any human's should. The thick greasepaint melts into his face, and the natural peach color shows through. "I don't want you to forget it." He smiles in his red striped suit, but more terrifying without the blackface. "I want you to tell every bigot you know what you've seen."

Uncle Herschel pulls up his sleeve. His forearm bears a thin green tattoo of numbers, his concentration camp registry.

"I died in Auschwitz. We all died at one of the camps."

The other performers gather behind Uncle Herschel. He brings the point of his dagger to my jugular. The tip nicks my throat, and I feel a drop of blood roll down my neck.

"Give me your arm."

Uncle Herschel snatches up my right arm and pulls up my sleeve. He puts the tip of the blade against my skin and carves three numbers into it. I cry from the pain and terror. Through my tears, I watch 845 scab over without losing a single drop of blood.

"Let this be a reminder that you survived a holocaust."

I close my eyes because I cannot look at him anymore. My arm aches from the cuts. I hear his laugh, then the rest join in. Tambourines and banjos play an old church song, "Shall We Gather at the River." The air grows cooler, and the sweat sticking my clothes to my body chills me.

I open my eyes and find that I'm sitting in the middle of the empty fairground. The tent is gone as are any signs that Uncle Herschel's show ever came to town. My ankle doesn't hurt, so I stand. Sure enough, there is no pain. I turn and walk to the parking lot. My car sits alone under the only working street light.

As I walk through the gate, I stop and roll up my sleeve. Underneath the cotton, *845* stares back at me as a thin green tattoo.

I run across the parking lot and clamber into my car. When the engine roars to life, my radio blares out the last station I had it on. Elvis sings his "American Trilogy" at the part where he is looking away from Dixieland. I turn it off and take a last look at the fairground. On the placard at the gate, an old poster, almost faded away to nothing, stares at me from under the light hanging on the ticket booth. In

Halloween orange letters, it announces Uncle Herschel's Traveling Old Time Minstrel Show, with a label in dark red lettering across the bottom stating, *cancelled August 1945.*

Somewhere I hear a tambourine jingle and smell the mixture of blood, vomit and excrement. I drive away tossing up dirt and gravel behind me.

Pabst Blue Ribbon Moon

Marissa watched Simeon as they drove south on Interstate 65, heading for their spring break vacation. She couldn't believe it. She and Simeon Wolfe, the hottest man she'd ever known, much less dated, would be sharing a room for a whole week.

She'd never spent an entire week alone with Simeon. To think of it, he'd only stayed the night with her maybe three times during the six months they had been dating, and she had never stayed with *him*. It surprised her when he asked her to go to his family's condo in Florida—and on the way down, to stay the weekend on their farm somewhere in way-back Alabama.

A McDonald's emblem blazed on the green reflective paint of an exit sign. They'd not eaten anything since leaving Nashville.

"You think we can pull off and get a bite to eat?" she said.

Simeon's blue eyes sparkled. He looked at the clock on the stereo. "It's not that long until nightfall."

"We can't eat until after dark?"

"My mom's cooking a big supper for us this evening, and I told her we'd be there before the moon rose with a ravenous appetite."

The late afternoon sun that shown through Marissa's window caught the highlights in Simeon's short cropped hair. His strong jaw flexed.

"What's the matter?" she asked.

"Just nervous."

"I'm sure I'll love your parents, and I know that they'll like me." She played at being overly narcissistic. It always got a chuckle.

Simeon stared at the traffic ahead and gnashed his teeth.

"Want me to flash you?" she asked. "That might calm you down."

A small grin stretched across his lips. "That'd be okay."

"Well, I'm not. I don't want you wrecking before we get to the beach. I don't want to spend my spring break in..." She gazed out the window at the passing road sign. "Evergreen, Alabama."

"It's not that bad of a place. Not really a spring-break destination, though."

Now *she* smiled. He hadn't said much since the trip started, but he seemed to be loosening up. Usually, she couldn't get a word in edgewise with him.

"What's got you so worried?" she asked.

"Full moon's tonight."

Marissa hadn't realized it was the full moon. Simeon told her that he had a rare disorder where the intensity of the gravitational pull of the full moon gave him severe migraines. He'd hole up in his apartment for three nights, wouldn't answer the phone or reply to text messages. He claimed there was no medication for it.

"Are you already feeling a migraine coming on?" she asked.

"Not yet. They don't start until the moon comes out. That's why Momma's expecting us before then. She knows I can't keep anything down once I get one."

"This is going to be interesting, Mr. Wolfe. I'm finally going to get to see you on a full moon. Who knows, it might bring out the beast in me."

"I'll be locked up in my bedroom tonight. I can't stand lights or noise. I can't describe how bad this ... these headaches get."

Marissa had migraines occasionally, a symptom of a really bad cycle. She didn't remember them being quite *that* bad, though. She remembered her grandmother would go numb on one side when she had a "sick headache."

"Does anyone else have migraines like you?"

Simeon nodded as he took the exit off the interstate. "My dad gets them really bad. My sister and brother too. I guess they run on my dad's side. The Wolfe side."

***

A deep orange light hung over the tops of the pines as Simeon and Marissa drove down the gravel driveway to the Wolfe farm. They drove over a small bridge, and Marissa watched water swirl around rocks in the shallow stream that cut across the front fields. The house loomed over the fenced-in yard with a flagpole in the middle. The flag blew in the light wind, its colors glowing in the dying light.

Simeon parked, and Marissa climbed out and stretched. The air chilled with the growing twilight. A flood light flickered on, bathing the flag in bright white.

The deep musk of animals filled her nostrils. Somewhere, wood smoke penetrated the other odors with its gamy smell.

She took a chance to study the façade of the house. It might have been from the set of some old Civil War movie. The driver's side door slammed, and she looked over at her boyfriend. He smiled.

"We're here."

"Yes, we are."

She walked around the back of the car and hugged him. He put his arm around her, but then pushed her away.

"We need to get the stuff out and into the house." He popped the trunk open.

Marissa tried not to feel slighted as she pulled out two small periwinkle suitcases. Simeon reached past her and jerked out his black gym bag. He smiled as he took the larger of her two bags from her.

"I figured Rueben would be here by now," he said.

"Your brother is coming in from Troy?" she asked. "They have spring break the same time as we do? You should have invited him to go with us to the beach."

Simeon pushed down on the trunk lid. "He's not on spring break. He always comes home at the full moon."

Marissa picked up her bag and followed Simeon up the brick steps, to the gate, and into the yard. It seemed strange that his brother would drive all the way home just because of migraines. Troy University wasn't as far away as Vandy, but it still seemed inconvenient. "Why does he do that?"

"He lives in the dorm. Getting away from the noise and lights would be hard. If he stayed, it would be miserable for him." Simeon pushed past her and up the steps to the large front porch. "I used to do the same thing when I lived in the dorms my freshman year."

"You drove all the way from Nashville once a month for a year?"

He sat her bag down on the plank floor and rang the doorbell. "Yeah."

The door opened. A women with Simeon's eyes smiled out.

"Momma." He hugged her. "Momma, this is my girlfriend, Marissa Ross." He turned, smiling to Marissa. "This is Momma."

"You can call me Mrs. Wolfe or Darlene. It's your choice." She stuck out her hand.

Marissa took it. Mrs. Wolfe shook hands like a man: hard grip and powerful up and down motion.

"Nice to meet you, Mrs. Wolfe."

She took Marissa's bag and pulled Simeon through the door. "I can't believe y'all came on a full-moon weekend."

"I figured we could get here before moon rise," Simeon said.

Marissa stepped into the house's entryway. A staircase disappeared to the next floor, and a grandfather clock with a large crescent moon carved into the top sat in another corner. The whole place smelled like fried chicken.

"Supper smells good," Simeon said.

"Fried chicken, mashed potatoes and biscuits—your favorite," Mrs. Wolfe said, closing the door behind her. "I figured that it'd be a good meal for everyone." She looked at Marissa. "You like fried chicken, don't you, sweetie?"

Marissa nodded. "Oh yes, that'll be fine."

"Y'all come on into the kitchen. I'm just finishing up. You can help me get the table set." Mrs. Wolfe walked down the hall and into the next room.

Simeon took Marissa by the hand and followed. The hallway opened into a large living room. A sectional sofa took up most of the central floor space. Three large portraits covered one of the walls. She recognized a younger Simeon dressed in a tuxedo with a black bowtie. A girl with shoulder-length hair and a black velvet collar was in the middle picture—she looked like Simeon. The last picture was of his brother, Reuben. She'd seen pictures of him in Simeon's apartment.

"Those are our senior portraits," he said. "You've probably never seen a picture of Dinah. I don't keep any of her around. I don't like for my buddies up at Vandy to see her. They always want me to hook them up with her."

"Why not?" Marissa asked.

"Have you met my buddies?"

They laughed as they walked into the next room. A dining table sat between the wall and a counter bar with several oak chairs surrounding it. Mrs. Wolfe stood in the kitchen on the other side of the bar with her head stuck in the oven.

"Biscuits are almost ready," she said, turning out to face them. "Go ahead and start setting the table."

"How many places do we need, Mrs. Wolfe?" Marissa asked.

"Six."

"Why so many?" Simeon asked. "Is Reuben bringing somebody with him?"

Mrs. Wolfe took the biscuits out of the oven. "No, Dinah's coming home this weekend."

"All the way from Ole Miss?" Marissa tried not to sound so surprised. "Is she on spring break too?"

"She's started coming home on the full moon since moving into her sorority house. She can't get a moment's peace. We told her not to do it, to stay in her apartment, but you know her."

"These must be some horrible migraines your children have, Mrs. Wolfe."

"Migraines?"

"Yes, Momma. You know the full moon causes us all to have horrible headaches," Simeon said.

Mrs. Wolfe fluttered her hand and screwed her eyes up like she'd just remembered something. "I don't know what's gotten into me. We don't usually call them migraines, Marissa dear. We call them moonaches, and have for years. I had a slip of memory."

"I think I'm starting to feel a twinge of one now," Simeon said. "Could you go get me an Excedrin from the bathroom, Marissa? Go back into the hall and take the door by the clock."

Marissa walked away. She found the bathroom and probed into the medicine cabinet until she found the green bottle of migraine medicine. She took the whole bottle back with her. As she came to the doorway into the dining room, she stopped and stood in the shadows. Simeon and his mother whispered on the other side.

"I can't believe you haven't told her the truth," his mother said.

"Believe it or not, I'm not sure she'd take it well. I mean think about other girlfriends who have found out. A few of them almost died."

"Don't be so dramatic. You know that I've tried to protect every girlfriend and boyfriend you and your brother and sister have had."

A hand took hold of Marissa's shoulder. She jumped and dropped the bottle of Excedrin.

"I'm sorry." The voice was deep, almost a growl.

Marissa turned around and looked into the deep blue eyes of an older version of Simeon. He smiled, showing long white teeth.

"I didn't mean to scare you," he said. "I'm Jake Wolfe. You must be Marissa, Sim's gal."

"Yes, sir," she said, trying to sound relaxed and at ease.

Simeon came through the door. He looked at his dad and then at her. She saw the look in his eyes and felt guilty.

"I was about to sneeze," she said. "I stopped to keep away from the dinner table." She smiled back at Jake Wolfe. "I guess you scared it out of me."

"I knew that would stop hiccups, but I never heard of it handling sneezes," he said, still smiling. "We got the table ready, Sim? I just saw Dinah and Reuben pull up."

"We're all ready."

"Good. I like to get finished eating before the moon rises." He handed Simeon the bottle of medicine after picking it up from the floor. "I hope your headache isn't already starting."

Simeon rubbed his temple with his empty hand. "I'm feeling a little tension pain."

"Better take some of those pills then." He patted Marissa on the shoulder. "Let's get on in there and get everything ready. Reuben comes in like a ravenous tornado and might eat the table otherwise."

***

Marissa sat a pile of plates down beside the sink. Mrs. Wolfe turned off the water. Suds frothed to the rim of the sink. Jake, Dinah, Reuben and Simeon sat around the table.

"Are you sure you don't want me to help you wash the dishes?" Marissa asked.

"No, go spend some time with Simeon and the others. You won't see them again until tomorrow morning sometime. They'll sleep late. Those headaches always take their toll on them."

Marissa walked back to the table. She started to scoop up the knives, spoons and forks. "Can't forget the silverware."

Everyone at the table hissed at her like each had been slapped on a fresh sunburn.

"We don't call it that," Mrs. Wolfe said from the kitchen.

"I'm sorry." She tried to keep the confusion out of her voice.

"We call it flatware," Jake said. "It's bad luck to say silver."

Marissa walked back into the kitchen and set the flatware beside the plates.

"It's an old Gypsy thing," Mrs. Wolfe said. "I'm the only one that will say it without cringing. I'm also the only one who will wear it."

"So you are of Gypsy descent?" Marissa asked.

"We prefer Romani to Gypsy, but yes," Jake said.

She walked back to the dining table and sat beside Simeon. "You never told me that."

"You never asked."

"Can you read palms and that sort of thing?"

Dinah made a *psst* noise and rolled her eyes. "That is so cliché."

"It may be, dear, but we can do it," Jake said. "Mind you, it's not a genetic thing." Everyone at the table chuckled. "It's a learned behavior, part of our culture."

"Just like stealing babies and swindling people," Reuben said.

"Hush," Simeon popped his brother on the back of the head. "We don't really steal babies."

Marissa patted him on his hand. "I know that, but I never knew you could tell fortunes."

"Sim is good with palms," Jake said. "Reuben reads the tea leaves, Dinah's an expert with the bones, and I use the Tarot."

"You're pulling my leg," Marissa said.

Jake looked at the clock over the stove in the kitchen. The black cat, whose tail flicked and eyes blinked the seconds, said it was 7 p.m. Marissa could see through the kitchen window that the night had come on, but the moon had not risen.

"We have just enough time," Jack said. "I'll get my deck. Dinah get some of the leftover bones from supper, and Reuben, get Marissa a cup of tea."

Jake left the room, and the two others gathered their items. Simeon sat with both hands on the table. He drummed his fingers.

"I don't think this is a good idea," he said to no one in particular.

"Why not? It'll be fun," Marissa said.

"For you perhaps, but I can feel my headache starting."

"Come on, Sim. She's got to learn about us sometime," Dinah placed a plate with several chicken bones on the table.

"Especially if she's going to stick around," Reuben put a tea cup with steaming water in front of Marissa. He set a tea bag beside her. "Go ahead and start dipping."

"No really, we should save this for tomorrow, or never," Simeon said.

"Son, she's going to find out one way or the other," Mrs. Wolfe said.

"We still have nearly an hour yet," Jake said as he walked back to the table. He shuffled a deck of cards. "Dinah, you start."

Marissa let her fortune be told. She first did what Dinah instructed and found out that a great mystery would be revealed to her, but the bones could not say what. Next, Reuben read her tea leaves. He saw a fuzzy glimpse into the future. Love would either grow stronger or weaker, he couldn't tell. He decided that he should have used Earl Grey instead of Lipton. Marissa let Jake read her cards. She drew five: death, the lovers, the two of swords, the devil, and seven of coins.

"I don't like the look of those," she said.

"Do not worry. Things are often different than what they seem," Jake said. "Everyone worries when they get the devil and death, but those, in your case, are positives."

Marissa looked down at the figures printed on the cards, every one of them wolf-like in appearance. Death wore a black cloak, but his hand was furry and clawed. The lovers were two rampant dogs, and the devil was a wolf in sheep's clothing. All had dripping, ravenous fangs. Jake stared into the cards as if reading a great novel.

"Tonight, you will have the secrets of love revealed. All the questions will be answered." He looked at her and smiled. "The cards say love will grow stronger, and your life will change forever. That's what the death card means."

"For better or worse?" Marissa asked.

"The devil would say for worse, but he is upside down, so probably for the better," Jake said.

Marissa bounced in her seat. She was happy to move away from the disturbing cards and let Simeon read her palm. She held out her right one. He shook his head and folded her fingers back to her palm. His touch felt cold as he pulled her left hand forward. She opened it.

"I don't want to do this," he said.

"Go on, everyone else has. It's fun," she said.

He looked at his family, one at a time. Marissa did the same. Mrs. Wolfe nodded her head in approval, and Simeon licked his lips and stared down into Marissa's palm.

"I see that you will have a change tonight. You will never be quite the same." His hand started to shake as he held hers. "I … I can't go on."

"Please," Marissa said.

"Yes, son, it is ill luck not to finish a reading," Jake said.

"I can't. Don't make me."

"Go on, you wuss," Reuben said.

Simeon looked at his mother and then back at her palm. His hand became clammy as it held hers.

"I see the pentagram."

Everyone at the table gasped. Simeon let her hand fall to the hard wooden surface. He pushed away from the table and stormed out of the room. Reuben and Dinah followed him. Marissa looked around, first at Jake, who looked thunderstruck, and then at Mrs. Wolfe, who had sympathy in her eyes.

"What is it?" Marissa said. "I don't understand. What's happening?"

Jake stood up. "There's about fifteen minutes until moon up. I'm going to help the kids out. You know what to do, dear."

He left. Marissa wanted to jump up, grab Mrs. Wolfe, and shake her until something made sense. Everything inside her seized with icy fear. Mrs. Wolfe hurried to the table and lifted Marissa up.

"Wear this." She took off a necklace with a silver charm in the shape of the Confederate Battle Flag and handed it to her. "Keep it on from now until I tell you otherwise."

Marissa pulled the necklace over her head. "I don't understand. Please, tell me what's going on. I'm scared. Have I done something wrong?"

"No." Mrs. Wolfe pulled her away from the table. "We've got to get you to your room, and whatever you do, don't come out until tomorrow morning."

Marissa walked with her. "What if I need the bathroom?"

"There's a half bath in the bedroom."

"Why won't you tell me what's happening?"

Mrs. Wolfe stopped and pulled Marissa to face her. The older woman's eyes glowered with heavy seriousness. "If you don't do exactly what I've told you to, you won't be around to worry about needing the bathroom."

***

Marissa tossed and turned under her covers. Too much light shined into her room for her to sleep. The moon seemed extra bright tonight. Perhaps it shined brighter in the country, she thought, turning her back to the window.

Two o'clock stared at her from the digital clock on the bedside table. She'd lain down around midnight after reading the same outdated *Good Housekeeping* three times. Two hours of listening to her thoughts felt like an eternity.

A loud slamming echoed up from the ground floor. Marissa sat up. Her red sleeping shirt looked pink in the sickly yellow moonlight. Another door downstairs slammed. The bed shook from the force.

Marissa hurried out of bed. She rushed to the door and shook the handle. The door was locked, but something had to be going on. Was there a fire? She breathed in deeply, trying to detect smoke. The room smelled like eucalyptus and Comet.

A loud yell rose from below her window. Marissa abandoned the door and ran across the room to it. She pulled back the sheer curtain revealing the yard below. Several people ran toward the large barn at the back of the house. Marissa didn't recognize them. They hunched over, almost animal-like. One threw his head up toward the full moon and let out a howl.

It looked like Simeon, but that wasn't possible because of his migraines. She opened the window, and cool night air blew into the room.

"Simeon, is that you?" she yelled to the figure.

It looked up at her, let loose another howl, and ran after the others. Marissa caught a good look at his face. At that distance, she thought the howler was Simeon, although his features seemed ... different.

"Are you all right?" she yelled, but he kept running.

She watched the runners until they disappeared into the shadow of the barn.

What's going on here?

The lock on the door wouldn't give, and no ramming her shoulder into it would break it free. The window was the only way out, so she put on her shoes and crawled onto the sloping roof. The shingles were slick with age. She kept a hand on the wall of the second story to balance herself until she came to the corner. A latticework entwined with budding wisteria vines rose from the ground.

The little nibs of wisteria stems poked into her hands and legs as Marissa climbed down from the roof. Some of the limbs tangled with her clothing and tore it in places.

She started toward the barn. A choir of whoops and howls rose into the night. The smell of wood smoke wafted into the air. Her stomach knotted up. The full moon cast a jaundiced light over everything. Someone, or something, bayed at the moon.

Marissa's head danced with fear as she passed through the open pasture gate. The stronger smell of wood smoke brought her back to her mission. An orange glow vanquished some of the shadows at the side of the barn. Music filled the air. The twang of a honky-tonk piano mingled with the whine of a steel guitar. Some nasally singer warbled about whiskey and women. Another wolf-howl cried into the night.

"What are you doing here?" Mrs. Wolfe asked from the shadows as Marissa passed the corner of the barn.

Marissa yelled and grabbed her chest. "What are *you* doing here?"

"I'm making sure my family doesn't lose control," Mrs. Wolfe said. "It's my duty as their mother and wife."

"Why would they lose control?"

"They always run that risk during the full moon." Mrs. Wolfe grabbed Marissa by the arm and pulled her away from the barn.

"I don't understand."

"Where's the necklace I gave you? I told you to wear it all the time."

"I don't like Rebel flags. They're tacky."

Mrs. Wolfe shook her head. "You don't understand. It was your protection. Get back to the house before Simeon knows you're out here."

"Why should I care? He's my boyfriend."

A whooping howl came from behind the barn. Marissa recognized Simeon's voice. Mrs. Wolfe looked over her shoulder as she pushed Marissa back toward the house. The moonlight glinted off a silver Rebel flag charm hanging from a silver necklace around her neck.

"You've got on another of those necklaces," Marissa said.

"It protects me. Why do you think I'm not one of them? I've never taken it off since Jake's mother gave it to me."

"Somethin' smells good." Simeon's voice came crashing from around the barn. His accent sounded thicker than usual. "Momma, what am I smellin'?"

"Nothing," Mrs. Wolfe yelled back. "Just get back round there with your daddy and drink another beer."

Marissa saw Simeon's outline at the edge of the shadows. It looked different, more primitive.

"Naw, I smell a girl and *woo wee*, she smells pretty."

"What's going on?" Marissa almost cried.

"Yeee haawww!"

Simeon ran out from the shadows. His yellow teeth bucked out, and his hair rested on his shoulders, but only in the back. The top was short, almost a crew cut. He wore a flannel shirt with the sleeves ripped off. His arms were white from just above his elbows to his shoulders. The lower part was a rust color. As he drew closer, she saw that he had a Fu Manchu moustache and a stubble beard. The sweet smell of cheap beer emanated from him like stench from a skunk.

"Run!" Mrs. Wolfe said. "For goodness sake, run!"

Marissa did. She turned and dashed as quickly as she could back toward the house. Simeon whooped from behind her. She glanced over her shoulder to see him pursuing. Mrs. Wolfe yelled at them both, but Marissa couldn't make out the words. Her blood pulsed through her ears, deafening her to everything except the song Simeon sang: "Give me a Redneck Girl."

Before she could run through the pasture gate, he pounced. Marissa crumbled under Simeon's weight. She wriggled and tried to free herself, but it was no use. She felt his teeth against her neck and smelled his beer-laced breath. He bit down like he was giving her a hickey, and everything went black.

***

Marissa woke when something wet and icy touched her forehead. She grabbed it and pulled it away from her face. The blue and white label of a Pabst Blue Ribbon can glistened in the moonlight. A fire blazed a few feet from her. Simeon, still wearing his flannel shirt and his hair still in a glorious mullet, sat on a stump near the fire. He finished off a beer and crushed the can against his forehead. Jake and Reuben sat near Simeon. Both had long mullets and drank beer. Dinah danced near a boom box. Her bangs stood up high and didn't move as if set in place with the strongest hairspray known. She held a wine cooler in her hand. Conway Twitty serenaded the night.

"Put that beer on your bite, sweetheart," Mrs. Wolfe said. "It'll help with the fever."

Marissa looked beside her. Mrs. Wolfe rolled an opened beer can between her hands. She wore a downtrodden look of failure on her face. The silver flag pendant caught the light of the fire.

"What happened?" Marissa asked.

"He got you, just like he warned," Mrs. Wolfe said. "Now you're one of them, like it or not."

"What are they?"

"Were-necks," Mrs. Wolfe said. "Every full moon, they turn into rednecks for a three-day cycle. A hickey from them during that time will turn whoever receives it into a redneck too." Mrs. Wolf shook her head. "I tried to warn you."

Marissa only half-understood what Simeon's momma had said. Her head itched. She scratched it and felt the stiff puff of bangs piled high on her head. A sudden craving for Pabst Blue Ribbon overtook her, and she'd be danged if Conway Twitty wasn't the best singer in the whole wide world.

The Last Beautiful Woman

Vincent Price's *The Last Man on Earth* plays on the television. Of all the movie versions of *I Am Legend*, this one is the best. Price played Robert Neville to the hilt without his sometimes over-the-top acting. Every time, over the last forty years, that I've sat down to watch an old horror movie marathon on this night, I'm surprised that we still celebrate Halloween.

The beginning of the end started on Halloween night. By Christmas the whole world had changed. It didn't happen quite like Dr. Neville's story, but it was devastating all the same.

I was twenty-six that Halloween. It was a Tuesday, a horrible day for the holiday. No one wanted to have a party because of work the next day. Only the kids ever enjoyed a mid-week Halloween. It didn't matter what night the holiday fell on, trick-or-treat always came rain or moon shine.

My old neighborhood was in an up-and-coming part of town with plenty of young married professionals with kids. Soccer moms ran the place. I watched another horror movie marathon that night in between the numerous ding-dongs on the doorbell from ghouls and freaks wanting sweets. My treat was the crack cocaine of the candy world, Pixie Stix. I didn't care if parents hated the things. They weren't my kids so why would it matter if they got all hopped up on sugar and couldn't sleep.

The end credits for *The Fog* were rolling when my doorbell rang. I hoped this was the last of the spooks. My supply of sweets ran low, and besides, The Disney Channel was about to show *Hocus Pocus.* I hated being interrupted during that movie. It was a Halloween staple of mine in the old times. After three frantic dings of the bell, I grabbed my bowl and headed to the door. Through the frosted glass door, blurred shapes loomed mysteriously like a movie monster waiting to strike. When I opened the door, a green-faced witch with a broom in one hand and a black plastic cauldron bucket in the other yelled the mantra of Halloween. Her brother did the same but without the gusto. At first I thought his costume was a zombie, until I realized he wore a black felt hat with a skull and crossbones on his head. Engorged, green pustules pocked his face. His eyes drooped, blood shot.

"Is he okay?" I asked his mother who loomed at the bottom of the porch.

"Of course not, have you looked at him. He said something stung him as we walked up your sidewalk. He sneezed a few times right after complaining about the bite."

I dropped a few Pixie Stix in his bag and tried to hide the fact that the kid grossed me out. "Maybe this would be a good time to get him to the hospital."

"How many kids do you have?"

"None."

"Keep it to yourself then, Sally," his mother said. "Those bumps didn't come up until he knocked on your door. I'm a mother not a monster."

I almost reached into her kid's bag to take back my candy, but the boy's face moved. He didn't cause it. The boil-like things on his face pulsated. They quivered on their own. He reached to scratch at them.

"I wouldn't do that," I said. "It doesn't look like those things are going to stay closed much longer."

"Mommy, my face burns," he yelled, dropping his bag and turning to his mother.

"Let me see."

She bent and put her face so close their noses almost touched. That was when the beginning of the end started. He screamed. All the pustules burst at one time in a garish eruption of greenish bloody goop that splattered all over his mother's face and his sister. The green witch screamed and slapped at her face where the stuff landed. His mother toppled over backward off the porch, swiping and pawing her face to clear it of the stuff. I'd never seen so much pus and corruption come out of a human.

The little boy squalled at the top of his lungs. He clawed at his face and fell to his knees. The girl continued to scream. Their mother cried for help. I pulled my cell phone from my pocket and called 911. Before I finished, the horrible boils spread over the girl's chin where the pus landed. Their mother never uncovered her face.

It took the ambulance two minutes to arrive. By then, the mother's face spewed its pus all over the ground. The paramedics hopped out of the vehicle. The boy lay on the ground, unconscious. The mother screamed as more of the boils erupted. The girl cried holding her hands over her face.

"What's the matter?" the taller of the EMTs asked the girl.

"They hurt," she said.

"What's going on?" the short EMT asked.

"I don't know," I replied. These people might've been dying on my lawn, and there was nothing I could do. My words came out rapid fire from panic: "Those kids came to trick-or-treat. The boy said something bit him and caused him to break out in big green boils. Then they burst. The mother said the kid was bitten by some kind of bug. I've never seen anything like this. It's terrible, like a horror movie."

"Let me see your face," the taller EMT told the girl.

"No," she said.

"I can't help you if you don't," the EMT said.

The girl took her hands from her face. The boils pulsated. I could see them from the porch. They wouldn't stay contained long. The EMT pulled gloves from her pocket and snapped them onto her hands. She poked at the girl's chin. The pressure sent the green pus erupting out like a volcano. The EMT covered her face with her arm, but the stuff hit her. The young girl screamed, clawing at her face, before falling unconscious to the ground. Small green blisters broke out across the EMT's arm.

"This is some kind of outbreak," she told the other. "Get some gauze and let's wrap this before I spread the pathogen."

The EMTs took care to cover the blisters before loading the boy up on their gurney. Another two ambulances came and took away the girl and her mother.

I came out of this encounter unscathed and free of the disease, but not free from the pockmarks of witnessing the end of everything that I had known for twenty-six years.

The next morning, a banging on my door woke me an hour before my alarm. I crawled out of bed and wrapped my old bathrobe around me. When I got to the door, the person on the other side hammered it so hard I thought it might break through the glass.

"Hold your horses," I said. "Honestly, who goes around pounding on doors this time of the morning?"

A man dressed in black fatigues stood on the other side. He held a cylindrical metal object in his hand. Not a speck of joy or lightheartedness lived in that man's face. The stony seriousness looked like something that should have been hanging on a cathedral in Europe.

"Can I help you?" I asked.

"Are you Stephanie Nichols?" the man asked in a tone as serious as his face.

"That's me."

He pulled a picture from his shirt pocket and held it out to me. It showed the woman and her two children from the night before, the ones who started the whole mess of the end.

"Do you know these people?" he asked.

"I don't know what their names are, but I know them."

"How?"

"They came trick-or-treating at my house last night. The little boy had these bumps on him. They burst everywhere. I called 911 and waited out here until the paramedics arrived."

"So these people were here last night, and this is where the kid's face exploded?" the man asked.

"Who are you?"

"Agent Oscar, but you can just call me Oscar. My name's not important. What is important is that you witnessed the boy's face erupt, correct?"

"Correct. I also watched his sister's and mother's faces do the same thing"

"Did any of the expelled substance from those sores get on you?"

"No."

"Not even while you were assisting the family until paramedics arrived?"

"Hell, no, I wasn't about to get that stuff of me. You should have seen it," I said. "It was like something from a horror movie."

"Trust me, ma'am, we have seen it. At least 30 people have been infected since last night."

"What?"

He ignored me and looked around my porch. His gaze stopped on a green spot dried on the cement near the steps. I planned on mopping it up with pure bleach and maybe ammonia after work.

Oscar stepped off the porch and walked on the ground to the edge where it was. He held the cylinder over the stain. Purple light beamed from it. The dried green pus glowed as if it were made of smashed lightning bugs.

He grabbed a walkie-talkie attached to his lapel. "I've found some of it."

"Where are you?" a voice said back.

"1794 Firethorn Street. Also, the owner claims this is ground zero," Oscar said.

"We'll be there ASAP. Don't let the owner leave."

"Ten-four."

"Can I ask what this is about?"

"It's not my place to tell you that. I'm only supposed to find ground zero."

"And you've found it?"

"If this is where Liam Swindle exposed his mother and sister to X35, then, yes, I've found it."

"Can I put on some regular clothes?" I asked, feeling a little silly in my flannel Cookie Monster pants and old Color Run T-shirt.

Oscar nodded. I walked back into my house with my head spinning through the events of the previous night. I'd been unable to put the sight of it out of my mind; people's faces didn't simply explode. But theirs had, and I knew something had changed at that moment. Now, the mysterious Oscar made me feel that I could be caught up in some kind of conspiracy.

When I opened my bedroom door, I expected to find a giant eyeball staring at me like the old *Twilight Zone* television series. Instead, I found my bedroom strewn with discarded clothes, clean and dirty, all over the floor and furniture.

Since I wouldn't be going to work, I put on a pair of rumpled jeans, a David Bowie T-shirt, and pulled on a Pittsburgh Penguins ball cap to hide my tangled hair. By the time I made it back to my porch, a unit of men clad in black fatigues stood on my lawn and clogged the street. A large RV with a rotating satellite dish barricaded the road. It was a surprise that no helicopters flew overhead. More and more I believed the CIA was after me.

"This is her," Oscar said to the only person not in fatigues. She wore sky blue hospital scrubs.

"My name is Doctor Melton." She extended her hand and walked toward me. "I'm with WHED."

I took her hand, cold and clammy in mine. She looked through me with her steel blue eyes. For a moment, I thought she might be some kind of robot.

"WHED?"

"World Health Epidemiological Division," she said. "It's not important. Agent Oscar, light her up."

Oscar took out his purple light again. He stepped up to me and shined the light over my body. The beam scanned all my exposed skin. Nothing glowed like the stuff on the porch.

"How were you dressed last night when Liam Swindell exposed the world to X35?" Melton asked.

"Long sleeves. I get cold at night."

She looked at Oscar. "Get some techs to clean off any of the specimen into Petri dishes and then cleanse the porch. She's not a threat." Melton turned to me. "Can we go inside and talk a few minutes?"

"If you'll explain what's going on, yes," I said.

"I will."

I invited her inside. At that moment my entire life changed again. I became one of the first civilians to know about X35 outside of the hospital staff where the Swindle family had been taken.

Dr. Melton perched on the edge of the couch as if afraid it might be infected with some unknown bacteria. She was an epidemiologist I told myself, trying not to take offense to the insinuation I was a bad housekeeper. She looked pretty in my house as I sat across from her. Outside, the harsh sunlight had blanched her out. In the warm glow of the living room, her femininity showed as brightly as the green goop under the purple light.

"What is going on?" I asked.

"According to reports, the boy's face erupted on your porch last night while he was trick-or-treating," she said.

"I've already acknowledged that with your Agent Oscar."

"EMT reports state that he was bitten by an insect near your house."

"I didn't witness that, but I remember his mother saying he was having an allergic reaction to a bug bite. By the look of his face, I figured it happened at least an hour before he got here. I couldn't imagine a reaction happening that fast."

"That's because it wasn't an allergic reaction. I've seen his mother and his sister. The pustules wouldn't result from a form of dermatitis."

"How does this involve me?"

Dr. Melton talked to me as if I were a colleague. I hadn't the foggiest idea about her medical chatter. A rash was a rash, and face full of green zits was a face full of green zits. She stared at me for a moment, and then a light bulb seemed to go off in her head.

"The bug infected him with a RNA restructuring proto-virus like we've never seen."

"Again, I need to know this for what reason?"

"This thing is going to kill humanity if we don't stop it," she said. "The boy has hours left. His mother might have a day. The girl less than a week. We, as a species, have no immunity for this thing. This is ground zero. If there really was an insect and it bit the boy near your home, it may still be nearby."

"That's comforting."

"Have you seen any strange bugs lately?"

I thought hard. It was the first of November. Most bugs skedaddled after the first good frost. Ladybugs invaded my house every year around that time, but they were as innocuous as water.

"Ladybugs," I pointed around to the spots they hung out mostly in the corners of the windows.

Dr. Melton followed my finger. I gazed up there as well, mostly to see how many milled around over each other. Not a single red and black bug moved on the window. It was as if no insects had ever taken up residence there.

"Are these invisible ladybugs?" she asked. "Or are you screwing with me? This is important work. Thirty nurses and lab techs at Greenwood General have become infected from simple exposure to the pus even while using advanced contact precautions similar to that used for Ebola. If we don't find this bug, the entire hospital will be quarantined if not the whole town. Bugs have a way of biting more than one person."

"I'm not joking," I said. "There were at least a hundred ladybugs on those windows last night when I went to bed. They die off quickly, but their husks are left on the floor or the windowsill. There's nothing. I can't explain it."

Dr. Melton took her walkie-talkie and barked an order into it. Agent Oscar and another large over-steroided looking fellow hurried in. They stood at attention, waiting for the doctor's orders.

"Agent Oscar, scan those window frames. Agent Romeo glove up and start searching for a bug in here," she said.

"What kind of bug?" the over-muscled man asked.

"One you don't recognize, something alien," she said. "Don't get stung."

The two agents searched my house. The purple light found traces of the green stuff on my windowsills. Small spots of the stuff not visible to the naked eye clustered in the corners where most of the ladybugs usually milled around. Agent Romeo came up short. The doctor gave no speculation about why the spots were found in the window except that the bug might have eaten the ladybugs. She gave me a business card and told me if I found the alien insect or had symptoms of the disease to call her.

The news that night had an exclusive story about what they called a "virus of unknown origin" breaking out in the Greenwood Hospital. Seventeen people had been further infected since the initial thirty-three infected, and WHED, referred to as a government agency, had quarantined the entire facility. The prognosis was lethal to all who came into contact. They warned of the symptoms, what to look for and who to report to. There was no mention of the bug.

For a moment as I watched the news in the changed world, I wondered if WHED and Dr. Melton would help the newly infected or exterminate them. Everything I'd ever seen in movies or read in books about outbreaks sided with exterminate.

I decided to read in bed even though it wasn't yet six o'clock. All the thoughts of outbreaks piqued my morbid curiosity. I picked up Richard Matheson's *I am Legend* and climbed under the covers to read it again. I planned to finish the story before I dozed off. The chance never came.

As soon as my foot slipped beneath the sheet, a sharp pain radiated from my great toe like a hot needle had been shoved under the nail and then blown off with a shotgun. By instinct my foot shot from under the covers. I pulled it to my hands to cradle the pained extremity and check for damage. The culprit clung on like a barnacle.

A cricket thing with legs more like a spider and fangs like Dracula stared at me from my foot with its multifaceted bug eyes. Its violet red and yellow color told me the thing was poisonous. No wonder the little boy looked as he had. This huge thing could have taken down King Kong.

The veins in my foot felt like molten lead flowed through them. They stood out from the skin, turning green as the bug's venom inched toward my leg. I reached down, pinched the thing behind its head and pulled it free. The fangs made an audible pop as they tore from my toe. The pain throbbed harder with removal of the bug, but the creeping fire and green coloration through my veins stopped, holding steady at the base of my ankle.

"How did that kid handle the pain," I said to the bug, half expecting the thing to talk back to me.

The legs walked in the air as I held it above me. The fangs turned under its mouth. Mandibles covered them. It clicked its jaws like the clacking keys of a typewriter. I stood with the thing wriggling in my fingers, completely alien to me. When my right foot hit the floor, searing pain struck as if every bone in my body were breaking in slow motion. It shot up my leg all the way to the top of my head. My foot flew from the floor. The shift of my weight sent me toppling to the ground. My hand hit the floor hard, opening my fingers and releasing the horrible little bug from my grasp.

We stared into each other's eyes mere inches away. Its eyes were so large I could see myself a hundred times locked in the faceted vision. It clicked its mandibles at me and shuddered. Green and blue wing-like things stretched from between its front mantis-like arms. The thing did a dance. It was a victory dance, I told myself. The horrible bug readied itself to strike my face with a killing blow.

Weakened by the venom, I had only one option. I puckered my lips and blew. The insect paused its dance and stared at me, tipping its head to the side like a confused dog. I blew at it again, harder this time, forcing out all the wind I had in my lungs.

The thing shuddered. The wings disappeared. It clicked a fearsome beat at me, turned and skittered away. My breath felt short. The venom moved toward my lungs. They burned not from the exertion but from the venom. My phone sat on the bedside table. I couldn't get to it. Death would take me in my bedroom, alone. No one would know. They'd find me months later rotted to skin and bones. As I thought I would draw my last breath, I remembered my phone was set for voice command.

"Phone," I barked.

"Yes, my lady," it replied as I had instructed it on one of my funnier days.

"Call 9-1-1."

"Dialing."

The phone began to ring. The dispatcher came on. I shouted my address first thing and then that I needed help. Before my voice slipped to nothing but a wind, I barked the address again. Everything turned green followed by black.

I awoke days later in an ICU bed under a plastic tent. The first thing I saw was a nurse looming over me dressed as if he had readied himself for a trip to Mars. The sight dried my mouth worse than it already was. He nodded when he saw that I was alert. I tried to move my hands, but cloth restraints secured them to the bed.

"What's going on?" I asked.

"You are in the hospital," the nurse answered with a voice garbled by his breathing apparatus.

"I know that," I answered. "I asked what's going on?"

"You are infected with X35 pathogen," he said. "I'm Greg, one of the staff trained to treat people with this disease."

"People?" the word rolled out as my tongue peeled from the rough of my mouth. "How many people?"

"Here or worldwide?"

"Worldwide?"

"This thing is a super bug. It has swept across the world. So far you're the only person to survive it," Greg said.

Everything inside me sank. The entire world crumbled before a pathogen. I alone survived. A tsunami wave of guilt crashed over me. Why had I been spared? What made me so special?

"Why?" I asked.

"We don't know. The doctors have been waiting to see if you would wake up before they began studying you," Greg said.

"Dr. Melton?"

Greg snapped his fingers. He walked to a speaker and pressed a button on it. A few moments later, Dr. Melton walked into the room dressed out like the nurse.

"Look who woke up," she said.

"Why?" I asked.

"Why did you wake up?" Dr. Melton asked.

I nodded. Fatigue grew on me, and words took too much effort. She shook her head. I didn't like that answer, but I supposed it was the only answer I would get. Dr. Melton took a long syringe from a drawer.

"I'm going to draw some blood."

Greg tied off my arm. I tried to make a fist but my strength was gone. She pushed the needle into my arm. Dark red blood almost purple sucked into the tube. Green globules floated in the blood like polka dots of disease.

"Do I have the sores?" I forced the words out with the last of my reserve energy.

"No, but the pathogen is in your blood," Melton said.

I wanted to say more but my head tingled. The room shifted one way then the other. Everything melted in front of my eyes. The room streaked down. Dr. Melton and Greg became flesh-colored smears. My body flung up in a convulsion. The needle ripped from my arm. Dr. Melton pushed me down to the bed. Another convulsion thrust my body into contortions, and everything went black.

***

My eyes fluttered open. The room looked the same. The machines whirred and beeped like they had before I passed out. A nurse walked into my vision dressed in an astronaut-like suit. The glare from the lights on the plastic shield obscured his face.

"Greg?" I mustered the voice.

"No, I'm Tom. Greg's been gone for a while."

"Shift change?" I asked, surprised by my own clarity of thought.

Tom shook his head. The giant headdress he wore didn't move, but his face moved from side to side within it. I knew he meant Greg was dead. Everyone I knew was probably gone.

"He died in the second wave," Tom said.

"How long have I been out?"

"About a month."

"How many waves?" I asked.

"We're in the third. The first was the worst. You woke up during that. About 1.5 million died in that wave. The second wave killed around 450,000 more. "

"Are they coming back?"

"The dead? No, this isn't the zombie apocalypse. They're calling it the Orange and Black Death since it started on Halloween."

"I know. I was there," I said.

"How did you contract it?" the nurse asked. "According to the notes left by Dr. Melton, you had no contact with the pus from the boils."

"A big ugly bug bit me."

"Just like the little boy," Tom said.

"Just like him." My mind went down a million garden paths at once. "How have you survived?"

He held out his arms and made a turn like a model on the runway. If his mouth hadn't been obscured by the breathing apparatus, he would have had a sarcastic smile.

"This thing protects me pretty well. I spend most of my time in one or in our clean room," he said. "The vaccine helps too. Dr. Melton synthesized one before she died at the beginning of the third wave."

"From my blood?"

"Yeah."

"Why am I still in isolation?"

"Because you still carry the pathogen in your blood. The vaccine doesn't work on you."

I looked over and saw my reflection in a mirror. My face looked clear as it ever had. None of the pustules had formed.

"If the vaccine cured the plague, why was there a third wave?"

"The deadliness of the plague was gone once the third wave began. The vaccine doesn't prevent the disease. It just keeps us from dying."

"What happens?"

"We still get the sores. They leave us looking horribly scarred and hideous. Every single person on the planet looks like a monster, except for you. You are the only *human* left."

I looked at myself again. Nothing about my looks had changed except a paler complexion from months in the hospital, and sunken eyes for the same reason, but at that moment, all the body image issues I'd ever had slipped away.

Tom stepped into the airlock outside my room. He returned with a wheelchair. My legs wobbled as they touched the floor for the first time after months of lying in bed. He helped steady me and then aided me to sit in the chair.

"What's going on?" I asked.

"The doctor said to move you as soon as you came to," he said. "Today is your lucky day. You're moving out of isolation into a regular room so that we can rehab you and get you back into the world."

A flurry of butterflies broke out in my stomach with the short ride from my bed to the airlock. When the door to my isolation room closed and the room pressurized, I almost jumped up with excitement. A woman dressed in a yellow paper gown with purple gloves walked in from the other door. She wore a paper hood and surgical mask. Only her eyes and brow showed.

"This is Marion," Tom said. "She's my partner nurse. After she helps me change, she'll assist you."

"Hello," Marion said, her voice muffled by the mask.

I watched her help Tom defrock. When his isolation hood came off, he wore one of the paper ones beneath it like Marion. I didn't get a look at his face before he put on the surgical mask.

"Am I still contagious?" I asked when he did this.

"Why?" Tom's eyes lit up when he understood why I posed the question. "No, we're not allowed to wear the other masks in the hospital. It's an infection control issue."

"Other masks?" I asked.

"Another time," Marion said. "Let's get you dressed."

She helped me out of the gown I'd worn for who knows how long and into disposable paper scrubs. A paper hood went over my head as well as a surgical mask. When I was dressed out, she pushed me into the next room. The sunlight coming through the window dazzled me. All I saw for a long time was the brightness of it. People and objects blurred by until I was in my room.

The next three weeks involved lots of physical therapy. Every day the therapists would come in dressed in paper hoods and surgical masks. They'd walk me around the room, but never let me out of it. Everyone who came in there dressed the same way. I only knew them by their voices and eyes. Every day, I grew stronger and closer to my caretakers until the day Tom came in with stack of papers and street clothes.

"Today is the day," he said.

"I get to go home?"

"The doctor has released you." Tom's eyes tilted up in what I had learned was a smile.

"Great."

"You just need to sign the papers and change into your street clothes." He handed me the papers and a pen.

It took me seconds to scratch out my signature. I was too excited to spend time with my careful writing. He took the forms and pen from me and stepped out so that I could change. The clothes he left weren't mine. They still had the store tags on them. I put them on anyway and then sat on the bed. Tom walked in pushing a wheelchair. He held a plastic bag in one hand. Without saying a word he handed it to me.

"What's this?" I asked.

"The last bit of your new wardrobe."

I pulled a plastic mask from the bag. It had ear pieces like eyeglasses and bent so as to cover the sides of the face. I looked at the front of it. Betty Boop stared back, with holes for eyes and a jaw that moved up on hidden hinges.

"What is it?"

"A mask," he said.

"I know that."

"It's for your safety."

I turned it over in my hands. Nothing would keep pathogens from my body like a surgical mask would.

"I don't understand."

Greg pushed my door closed. He peeled the paper hood from his head and slipped off the surgical mask. Underneath, I saw the ravages of the disease. His upper lip was gone, showing his teeth. Deep pockmarks pitted his cheeks. He put the mask back into place.

"Not everyone is going to be happy to see you, even if you saved their lives. That mask will keep you safe. Sorry about the Betty Boop, but they're the cheapest. I couldn't afford a good one."

I nodded and put the mask on securing the ear pieces. Greg replaced his hood and pointed to the chair. I climbed in, and we headed out into the hallway. As we passed patient rooms, I saw several Betty Boops looking at me. We rode the elevator with a man wearing a Dirty Harry mask. On the ground floor I came to realize how far things had changed. A mother with a gold-studded mask walked past holding her daughter's hand. The little girl's golden ringlets toppled over a Shirley Temple face. Another woman, older with a Chanel bag, wore a mask with the familiar double C logo. All the people bore the same blank stare of the stoic masks, uniform despite the varied patterns and adornments. The world became a sadder place for me at that moment.

***

Tonight I feel like Vincent Price as Robert Neville. I am what most people believe is an urban legend. I've lived the last few years alone in my apartment at the end of a very dark and lonesome street. I wear my out-of-fashion Betty Boop mask just like the rest of them when I happen to go out, never forgetting what Greg told me all those years ago. Only the people who live in my complex ever speak to me. None of them have the faintest idea that I am the woman who saved their lives.

Decades after the world changed, I thought humanity would have given up their masks, but they cannot stand the hideous things in the mirror. Face styles change, but no one ever walks outside without their human mask.

On Halloween kids still beg for candy. They still say "trick-or-treat" with glee like the time before the plague. The holiday will always exist as long as people need a good scare.

My doorbell rings. I grab my bowl of Pixie Stix. As I approach the door, I look at the aquarium on my bookshelf.

Ziggy Stardust prowls around in it. When I returned from the hospital all those years ago, I caught the bug that started the whole thing. It nested under my dresser, living off the fiber in my carpet. The thing is not of this Earth, so I decided it was a Martian spider. It snaps its mandibles at me.

The bell rings again with a manic rapidity.

Three horribly disfigured children stand at my door. Tonight's the one night of the year when they don't wear a mask. Each holds a plastic bag with a Frankenstein's monster painted on it, ready to receive the delicious treats.

"Trick or treat," they sing out.

I drop candy into their bags. Their mother decided to celebrate the holiday with her children. Her greenish pocked face smiles at me. Too much of her teeth show from where the pustules destroyed her lips.

"Thank you," the children say and head down the hall to the elevator.

"Wait," I say, putting my bowl of candy on the table just inside the door. "I haven't had my go yet."

The kids and their mother turn and look at me. I put my hands on my mask.

"Trick-or-treat?" I ask.

The kids look confused but grip their bags closer to them to protect their candy.

"Trick," the little boy says.

I pull the mask off, revealing an aged but unblemished version of a human they've only seen on old movies and TV shows. Their eyes, even their mother's, widen. One girl screams.

"Boo!" I yell, and laugh giddily as they run off.

I am an urban legend. The woman with a real face under her mask. The woman who saved the world. The last beautiful woman who shows her monstrous face only on Halloween.

The French

Dark gray mud squished over the top of Billy's boots. Every step made a sloppy, plopping sound as he trudged along the narrow path deeper into the woods. Poochie, his black and white terrier, pranced ahead of him, stopping occasionally to look and make sure his master followed. Birds chirped in the trees, and a few rustled in the fallen leaves on the side of the path. Billy stepped onto firmer ground. His little dog stopped and turned to the side of the path that led out into the swamp.

"Did you find one, boy?"

Poochie bounded into the shallows and splashed through the trees that stuck up from the brown water. Billy took his rifle from his shoulder and carried it across his chest so that he could aim quickly. He stepped off into the murky water. It covered the top of his muddy boots and chilled his feet through the thick rubber. He followed Poochie, never letting the dog get more than a few steps ahead. Over the splashing of the dog stalking through the water, Billy heard the frantic chatter of his prey. He spied a fat gray squirrel perched on the limb of a water oak. Poochie stopped at the tree and pawed up the trunk. He barked his high, yippy bark.

"Good boy." Billy aimed at the squirrel.

A small caliber bullet exploded from the barrel of the gun. Several limbs on the water oak shook, and dead leaves rained down in wads to the water below. The squirrel chattered louder and leapt to a sweet gum almost bare of its leaves. Billy fired again. A few of the serrated gum leaves floated down from the limb the squirrel rested on, but it jumped to another tree. Poochie gave chase, yipping and barking. He bounded through the water with great splashes. Billy followed keeping his rifle ever ready.

The squirrel jumped from a bare sweet gum tree into a gnarly post oak that had leaves hanging like sagging skin. Poochie bounded to the tree and pawed the bark. He yapped and snarled. Billy stopped short. Beyond the oak, he saw old mossy stones sticking up out of the ankle-deep swamp. One or two looked like crosses. He aimed and fired. The squirrel squealed, clambered around to the other side of the tree, and disappeared out of sight. Poochie dashed around the trunk to keep the chase. Billy knew he'd clipped the squirrel, but apparently not enough to kill it. Poochie didn't need to try and flush it.

"No, boy, come back. We can't go into the French. They'll be other squirrels."

The little dog glanced over his shoulder with an almost disappointed look but trotted back to his owner. The swamp water almost touched the dog's belly. Billy bent down and rubbed his black and white spotted head. The water on the other side of the post oak splashed. Poochie pulled away from Billy and ran to the oak again. Billy followed. He didn't need to lose his dog in the swamp.

The soil around the post oak felt firm under foot. Knots from the roots stuck up from the dirt. Poochie stood at the edge of the water that spread across the French. He stared toward a large green, mossy cross. Billy reached down and petted his dog again. Midway between where they stood and the tombstones, the squirrel bobbed up and down on the ripples.

"I guess I got a better shot on it than I thought, huh, boy?" he said to his dog.

Nothing else stirred in the French. No crickets chirped, nor frogs croaked. Birds didn't even land on the rocks jutting up from the stale water. The squirrel floated closer to the cross. Billy could read Le Fan chiseled into the stone. He glanced at the other headstones partially submerged in the swamp. Each bore a French name with lettering etched deep enough into the stones to withstand weather erosion. The old cemetery gave the place its name. No one went into it, and this was the closest Billy had ever come to it. For fifteen years, he'd heard stories around campfires at Halloween about why nothing went into the French. A curse was laid down to protect the cemetery from harm. The Indians in the area had cursed the place after their French allies, who had come up from the Louisiana colony, were massacred by British loyalists before the battle of Elizabethtown. The Cherokee in the area, like many other Indians, traded with whoever had the best stuff to offer. According to legend, the Frenchmen buried in the French offered guns and ammunition in exchange for furs and permission for French secret agents to cross their lands to assist the patriots.

All the Indian magic hadn't kept the cemetery from flooding, but it did keep everyone out—except for one unlucky, dead squirrel. Billy and Poochie watched the rodent float to La Fan's grave marker and then around to the back side of it. When the last wisp of tail disappeared, Billy petted his dog.

"All right, boy. Let's get on back. Maybe we'll pick up a few on our way home."

Billy turned and walked away from the post oak. Poochie followed him; then he pranced ahead on the path, running from side to side and sniffing the ground. Billy smiled and shouldered his rifle. As they put a few yards between them and the French, birds rustled in the trees, and a crow called out from somewhere deeper in the woods. Life flooded around him. Only then did Billy realize how quiet things had been. He looked over his shoulder and saw the post oak standing sentry over the old flooded graveyard, its bark covered with black moss and lichen. It looked like the Ferryman waiting to carry someone over to the other side.

Poochie barked his high-pitched call. Billy came to attention and drew his rifle from his shoulder. He ratcheted a bullet into the chamber. The little dog bounded off the trail into the woods. Billy followed. The pines that towered overhead choked off the brush and brambles so moving through the thicket was easy. The trees closed in around like a knot in a rope, getting tighter and tighter. Billy kept on Poochie's trail. The little dog weaved in and out of the trunks. He splashed through boggy patches; still, Billy kept on his trail. The last thing Billy wanted was go home empty-handed. His brothers would never let him live it down.

The trees started to open up. Branches quit pulling at Billy's clothes, and the drooping pine needles stopped brushing through his hair. He stood in a bare spot in the middle of the woods. A few trees stood here and there. A cowcumber tree with one or two giant brown leaves clinging to the limbs stood a hundred yards to the west. A sycamore with peeling bark marked the eastern point. A post oak stood sentry at due north like a black monolith. In the midst of all this, a single cedar tree kept silent watch. Poochie pawed his way up the trunk of that tree. He yipped and snarled up at the branches. Billy smiled and took a few steps closer. He looked for whatever Poochie had treed. The furry gray tail of a squirrel poked out from the thick green needles halfway up the cedar. The animal chattered and squawked down at the little dog.

"Good job, Poochie." Billy leveled his rifle ready to plug the squirrel. "You might be the best squirrel dog in the world."

His finger twitched on the trigger. He set his shoulder for the recoil when the tail disappeared over the side of the branch. A second later something jumped from the ground. Poochie squealed with pain. Billy watched as the little dog yelped and flung his head from side to side. All he could make out was a blur of black and white. Poochie quit flailing as the squirrel hit the ground. It clicked and chattered at the dog that started to growl and back off with his hackles standing on end.

"Get that squirrel!" He'd let Poochie kill this one, for revenge mostly.

The squirrel charged the little dog. Poochie fell to the ground with the squirrel hanging from his neck. Blood spewed into the air. The dog whimpered then lay still. Billy aimed his gun and blew the squirrel back several yards. Hunks of fur fluttered down like dandelion fluff. He walked to his dog. Blood covered the white fur and pooled around the dog's head. The squirrel had ripped out Poochie's throat.

What kind of squirrel does that?

A clucking sound came from the oak tree to the north. Billy looked up. The squirrel he'd just shot stared down at him from a low hanging limb. Its eyes glowed red as if it had coals in its sockets. It stood on three legs. Its right shoulder was nothing but raw meat. The fur around that wound matted with gummy blood. It charged him. Billy stepped to the side, and the gory vermin dashed by him. He chambered his last bullet. The squirrel turned. The devil eyes stared him down. It chattered again. *Rabid. It's got rabies.*

The dreaded disease was the only answer for such weird behavior, but it didn't explain why the animal kept coming with only three legs and fatal wounds. With a chatter-like war cry, the squirrel bound toward him again. The rifle roared. The animal somersaulted backwards a few times. It lay still on its back. Billy took his chance to get away from it. He left his faithful dog lying by the cedar tree and ran north.

Billy looked over his shoulder to see if the squirrel came after him. Nothing did, but he toppled over, slamming face first into the soft, mucky ground. Damp rotting leaves forced their way into his mouth. They tasted of death and decay. Billy sat up. He spat out the leaves and wiped the side of his face. The cool moisture of the ground soaked through his jeans. His ankle throbbed. He pulled his pants' leg up and rolled his grey sock down. His boot top ended at the bottom of his calf so he couldn't make out if his ankle was swelling or not. The boot felt like it was tightening around it, though.

Billy searched for what tripped him. A few feet from where he sat a jagged piece of limestone stuck up from the ground. As the dampness seeped into his bones, other slabs of limestone emerged from the background. Billy twisted to the tree that towered over the northern route, the black post oak that guarded the entrance to the French. Stagnant water eddied around it, and encrusted crosses stood vigil near the trunk.

Everything was quiet. The wind swirled in the trees surrounding the French, but not a gust ruffled a single leaf on the ground. Billy's heart echoed in his ears, louder and louder. He struggled to his feet, but as he applied pressure to his ankle, his leg buckled. He crumpled to the ground again.

The silence swaddled him. It tugged tight and almost cut off his breath. Then he heard it.

A chatter rose from the direction of the cedar tree. It echoed across the French, magnified fifty times by the unearthly silence. The scuttling footfalls of the small creature sounded like hoof beats. Billy saw the three-legged squirrel running toward him. The beady eyes glowed red. Its teeth shined white like fangs.

Billy scrambled to his feet, letting only the toes of his right foot touch the ground. He hopped on his good leg away from the charging squirrel. His rifle was nowhere to be found. The squirrel let out a noise like a rusty rake dragging across a slate chalkboard.

The squirrel drew closer as Billy hopped nearer to the edge of the swamp. His last hop buried his foot into the black, stinking mud. He struggled to free his foot but fell face first into the stagnant water. The chill of it took his breath but enlivened him at the same time. His foot came free in the fall. He moved easier in the water and pulled himself with his arms as he hopped on his good leg.

The squirrel stopped at the edge of the swamp. Its eyes reflected on the dark water. The horrible chattering continued, increasing in volume and speed. Billy waded as far as a slanted stone with *Louis Montcalm* etched into its face. His legs numbed in the chill of the water. The squirrel paced back and forth on the bank. Billy started to laugh.

"Can't get me; can you? I guess you'll have to go back to eating acorns."

He laughed again, and it boomed out across the French. It seemed that every headstone caught his laughter and amplified it. Billy glanced around as his ears filled with his own laughter, growing more and more sinister with every echo. He felt colder than ever. The French was supposed to be avoided at all cost. Never go into the French, the old ghost stories always ended. The laughter faded away, replaced by the rusty chatter of the squirrel. Billy looked to the bank, but the squirrel was gone.

Then the call came again, and he realized it came from above. Billy looked up. A long black limb of the post oak hung above his head. Brown leaves dangled from the smaller branches like rotting fingernails. Two red eyes glowed down at him, nestled in the bundle of leaves.

They rustled as if by a gust of wind, and Billy felt the weight of something smash against his head. He tottered and hit the corner of the tombstone with his temple. As the gleeful chattering of a playful squirrel echoed across his mind, Billy sank into the swampy water of the cursed cemetery. The foul liquid filled his lungs, and the old warning he'd always been told echoed within him: *Never go into the French.*

Strut and Fret Upon the Stage

Ramona looked at the building that matched the address on the advertisement. The place was a theater or had been at one time. Nothing had been performed at 3434 34th Street in a while. The marquee still hung over the entryway, but plywood covered the glass doors. It looked like a place where homeless people might put on Shakespeare but not a legitimate theater company.

The flyer said to knock upon arrival. Ramona's fist hesitated over the plywood. Despite the sense of dread in the pit of her stomach, she banged on the wood. If this production paid, she needed the work. Her last audition had gone horribly.

As she waited for what seemed like forever outside the boarded up theater, Ramona's mind drifted back a few days earlier. The audition almost traumatized her.

She had taken special care to learn everything about the character she read for. The lines had been easy enough to memorize. She even changed her hair color to match the character. Her time came to go on stage. She stood bathed in full light, unable to see the people for whom she auditioned out in the house seats.

"My name is Ramona Sparks. I played Anna in *The King and I* at USF while studying theater. I also had a minor part in *As You Like It* in last year's Shakespeare on the Pier."

"Very well," a voice said from the glare. "Lines, please."

She had stared into the nothingness, her mind a complete blank. Nothing came except her résumé spiel.

"My name is Ramona Sparks. I was Anna in *The King and I.*"

"We've been through that. Please say the lines."

Still nothing had come. She stood with a goofy grin on her face, completely blank in her mind.

"Thank you," the voice from the glare had said. "Natalie O'Nell, next."

As a heavyset woman, who looked nothing like the character description, waddled toward the stage, the lines flooded back in Ramona's brain. She began the monolog, but the director drowned her out yelling "thank you" until she'd walked off the stage. Too fat for the role, Natalie O'Nell did a perfect reading while Ramona, on the verge of tears, hurried into the alley behind the theater.

That's where she found the flyer for this audition. Apparently the producer was fairly savvy, knowing that freshly rejected actors would snap at any bait.

"Miss?" a deep, macho voice said.

Ramona focused back on the present. A ruggedly handsome man stood half framed in the opened doorway. His black hair shimmered like oil on water. His almost olive skin set off his glaring white teeth.

"Are you the producer of this?" she held up the flyer.

"I am and the director. You must have been at the audition at the Rialto on Tuesday," he said.

"I was."

He stuck out his hand. "I'm Guy Montgomery. Please come in."

The interior of the place shocked her. Despite the rundown façade, the lobby looked like a glittering movie house of years past. Gold shimmered from a chandelier. The ticket kiosk shined with new paint. The doors to the auditorium were made of dark lacquered wood with sparkling brass fixtures. Red velvet ropes cordoned off different areas of the lobby, including a stairway that led to a balcony and another area that had a door marked: STAFF ONLY.

"Wow," she said.

"I've been renovating this place from the inside out," Guy said. He pulled a book from beneath the refreshment counter which was void of the usual trappings of such an edifice. "What did you say your name was?"

"I didn't. I'm Ramona Sparks."

"Okay, Ramona. I can't audition you right now because I've already scheduled one at 10 am. I have time tonight about 7 p.m. Will that be okay?"

She would have to call into work, again, but she really needed a part. "Sounds good." She paused. "This isn't some kind of pornographic show, is it?"

Guy laughed as he jotted her name down in his book. "I wish. Those auditions would be awesome. This is a legitimate theatrical production. I need several young actresses. So you've got a decent shot."

Ramona thought she'd had a decent shot at the Rialto audition as well, but stage fright had other plans. She smiled.

"I hope so."

"I'll see you at 7 p.m. tonight." Guy walked back to the door to let her out.

"Do you happen to have a workable facility?"

He nodded and pointed to a lighted sign that said LADIES. Ramona hurried into the bathroom. It looked as updated as the rest of the place. The porcelain looked new. The fixtures were shiny brass like the handles on the auditorium doors. She did her business and washed up. A small purse lay on the marble counter. It was opened. Ramona peeked inside. Typical purse, lots of junk. A compact lay atop a feminine pad. There wasn't a wallet, but a small baggy of white powder stuck out from under the Kotex. For a moment, she thought about taking the stuff, but the last thing she needed was an angry cokehead coming after her.

Ramona dried her hands and walked out. Guy was speaking with his next audition, someone she instantly recognized: Natalie O'Nell, who had upstaged her at the Rialto audition. As Guy showed Ramona the door she tried to avoid eye contact with the other actress and not allow her derision to show.

"I'll see you tonight," he said.

"Okay, by the way, someone left her purse in the bathroom. You might want to call around and find who left it. I'm pretty sure she's going to want it back."

"Thanks." Guy almost pushed her out the door.

She heard the lock's tumblers click. It seemed odd to lock up behind her. Maybe he had a fat fetish and didn't want to be interrupted. Ramona flagged down a cab and headed to her job. She needed to change shifts with someone instead of calling in again. Her bank account couldn't afford it, and her manager's patience wore thin.

***

Suzanne's son ended up with explosive diarrhea at school. She had to pick him up and gladly traded shifts with Ramona, who secretly hoped that Natalie O'Nell got a dose of that particular ailment at her audition.

Ramona stocked a shelf with bodice-ripper romance novels. Her friend Misty stocked cozy mysteries on the other side of the shoulder-high shelf.

"We've not worked the same shift in a while," Misty said.

"I know. I like it better on evenings, less shelving. I always work the register or coffee shop." Ramona shoved three books by the same author into the shelf, but turned the cover's face out. "I like this writer."

"Not much goes on around here until lunch. Sometimes, I can slip out for a morning audition."

"I've got one tonight."

Misty showed her a book cover featuring a gray tabby cat dressed like Sherlock Holmes. "I can't believe people read these things. They look so corny."

"I know. Anyway, this play is at this place on 34th Street."

"The beat-up looking place with the fantastic interior?" Misty asked.

"Yeah, you know the place?""

"That's where I'm heading after work. Guy set up an audition for me today."

"Wouldn't it be great if we were cast together in the same play? He told me that he needed several young women in the cast."

"It would. You know my friend, Kara? She had an audition with him last night. She was supposed to let me know how it went, but I never heard from her. I bet she hooked up with him and forgot," Misty said.

"Isn't she the coke fiend?" Ramona squatted down to put books on a lower shelf.

"Yeah."

"I found a purse in the women's room. It had a bag of coke in it. You think it was hers?"

Misty blew a raspberry. "Who knows? Lots of women in this city snort coke. It helps deal with bad auditions and weight issues."

"It was a multicolored braided purse. There wasn't a wallet. I looked so I could find a contact number."

"Kara carries a purse like that." Misty stopped shelving and pulled out her cell phone. "I think I'll call her. It's not like her to forget her stuff, especially her blow."

Ramona finished putting the last few romances on the shelf while Misty called her friend. "So?"

"No answer. I texted her an hour ago and didn't get anything back either. She always texts back." Misty said. "Maybe they're still together."

"Can't be. I met with Guy today. She wasn't there."

"I'll have to ask about her when I go for my audition," Misty said. "Did he give you something to read from?"

Ramona shook her head. "He didn't say a thing about having a monolog prepared. I figured I'll do something from *The King and I*. It's my go-to reading."

They worked into the afternoon. When Misty got off, she promised to let Ramona know something about the play. About an hour after Misty left, Ramona received a text from her.

I'VE BEEN WAITING ON STAGE FOR 10 MINUTES. GUY JUST LEFT ME UP HERE WHILE HE TENDED TO THE LIGHTS. STILL NO IDEA WHAT THE SHOW IS ABOUT. MAYBE A MUSICAL.

Ramona texted back:

A MUSICAL?

After work Ramona headed over to the theater, even though she was an hour and a half early. Misty never responded to her message, which worried her. Misty was one of those people who made sure to follow through with her promises.

Ramona went into a small coffee shop just down the street from the theater. She ordered what she could afford: a regular coffee and a cold, day-old discount cheese Danish.

She sat at a table with a view down the street toward the theater. She texted Misty again.

As the street lights flickered on, the theater doors opened, and Guy ushered out a woman about her age, size and hair color. Her pouting face made Ramona nervous. Ramona checked her watch as time drew near for her own audition.

A waiter came with a coffee carafe.

"Need a warm-up?"

She smiled at him. "Thank you."

The waiter looked very nice. She could see him getting lots of tips with his square chin and deep blue eyes. His name tag read: Brad.

"I've not seen you here before," he said.

"I've never been here before. I'm waiting for an appointment," she said.

"Is it with Guy Montgomery?"

"Yeah."

"There's been like three girls in here this afternoon waiting for their auditions. I've got one with him tomorrow. I'm an actor too."

"We should run lines together sometime," Ramona said.

"If we get parts in his play, we'll be seeing lots of each other," Brad said.

She took a sip of her coffee. It was as hot as he was. "Guy said he needed several young actors."

"He told me the same thing." Brad snapped his fingers. "I bet it's *Seven Brides for Seven Brothers*."

"We could be married," she said. "My friend had an audition at 4:30 p.m. today. I've not heard from her and that's not like her at all. Have you seen her?"

"What did she look like?"

Ramona described Misty. He said two actresses who had come in around that time matched her description, but he'd not seen everyone that had gone for an audition. He'd seen even fewer leave.

The time came for her to go. Ramona tipped Brad a couple of quarters, and they exchanged numbers to follow up the auditions—and Ramona hoped a few other things.

The air had already cooled quite a bit since the sun had set. She walked the few yards to the theater. Guy flung the door open as soon as she knocked. A small frightened gasp escaped her. In the light spilling from the theater, his huge smile looked sinister.

"Did I scare you?" he asked.

"Surprised." Her heart pounded so hard she could hear it. "I didn't expect such a quick response."

Guy moved so that she could enter. "I was ready for you. My last audition ended rather quickly. The actress decided that the role wasn't for her. Thank you for being on time."

Ramona stepped inside. The lights from the chandelier glittered in all the polished brass fixtures. Guy had even turned on some of the neon signage. He locked the door behind her. The clicking of the tumblers echoed throughout the room and startled her again. Her fear instinct seemed to be in high gear tonight, and she hoped that wouldn't translate to freezing on stage.

"Sorry to keep scaring you," he said with his broad smile. "I have to lock the door. The boards keep people from smashing the glass, but it also welcomes vagrants to try and use the place. The façade looks like the perfect place to do *illegal* things."

"I understand. When I came here this morning, I thought the place was abandoned as well." She looked around. "So do I audition out here?"

"Of course not, the auditorium is that way," he pointed to the large wooden double door below a glowing green neon sign. "You can take the stage. I've got to turn on the stage lighting. There are steps to the stage on the side. Don't go beyond the apron. I've got everything beyond that point set up like I want it, and I don't need anyone accidently messing it up."

Ramona nodded and headed into the auditorium. The aisle sloped down to a broad stage. A white curtain separated the apron from the rest of it. As she stepped onto the hardwood planks, she took it all in. Never had she treaded the stage of such a grand place. Art deco sconces hung on the wall. Gilded cherubs smiled from the fronts of three private balconies on each side of the auditorium. In the house lights, the ceiling sparkled with crystals embedded in the plaster to look like stars. The stage remained dark. She wondered what was behind the white curtain.

"Life's but a walking shadow, a poor player that struts and frets his hour upon the stage and then is heard no more," Ramona recited in full theatrical voice. She wanted to hear the acoustics of the place.

"What was that?" Guy's voice boomed from the overhead speakers.

"I was just listening to the acoustics of the room," she said. "They're great."

"Just wait," his voice said over the speaker.

The house lights dimmed. The stage lights flared up. She looked behind her. Silhouettes that looked like dummies hanging in midair showed up behind the white curtain. Ramona took a step back. Her heel went off the edge of the stage. She caught herself before toppling over.

"You *are* jumpy, tonight," Guy said from the seats.

She turned. He wasn't visible in the glare of the spotlights.

"What would you expect? It looks like people hanging there."

"I'm sorry. I should have warned you, but you're the first to see this. I had no one's reaction to compare it to."

"So are those part of the show?" she asked. "Or are you a serial killer?"

"Both," he said matter-of-factly, then laughed.

The laughter sounded hollow in the blinding whiteness of the lights. A smell crept up that Ramona had not noticed earlier. The heat from the lights must have made it flourish. It burnt her nose enough to make her want to sneeze. The smell wouldn't take long to become noxious.

"So I'm assuming, you're not putting on *Seven Brides for Seven Brothers*," she said.

"Of course not. Why would you have thought that?"

"My friend Misty told me so," she lied. "She auditioned for you earlier today."

"I remember her. She was very good. I offered her a role on the spot. Why would she lie to you like that?"

"Maybe to put me off the production. She knows that I hate musicals," Ramona lied again.

"Well, lucky for you, we're doing a puppet show," Guy said. "Those things behind the curtain are my puppets. They'll always be in silhouette. It's very avant-garde."

"Do you have any lines for me to read?"

"No, improvise with the puppets."

Stage fright gripped her. She was horrible at improvisation. Even when she had lines, she would often miss a cue. Now she had to perform off the top of her head with giant creepy puppets that she could only see in shadow.

A beep echoed though the theater. The sound of grinding gears followed. The figures dangling behind the curtain moved their limbs. Like giant marionettes, the movements were herky-jerky, almost Frankensteinian.

"I'm operating them by remote," Guy said. "You can start anytime."

Ramona stood fast in silence. The movements were so artificial that she couldn't come up with any natural way to interact. The shapes looked human, but gender was unidentifiable. Nothing came to her. It was like that night at the Rialto; she had no idea where to go or what to do. The giant puppets moved in their *danse macabre*. A seat squeaked down below as Guy shifted around restlessly. She felt his impatience grow as intense as the spotlights.

The ice started to break off. Ramona moved about in a little half twirling dance with her arms trailing out beside her. She began to hum a childish tune as well. At first just random notes in a rhythm, but as she continued her twirl dance, the song morphed into "Ring Around the Rosie."

Guy made a low growling noise. "Can you do something besides that idiotic childish behavior?" he barked. "A three-year-old could do a better job."

"You're the director," she said. "How about some direction?"

"Use the space. Use the puppets."

"I don't know anything about them," she said.

"Then use your senses. How does it feel? Sound? Smell?"

That hit her just right. The stench came on stronger. It started to burn her nose, but she found inspiration. She remembered a poem from her high school English class, something with a Latin title that told about soldiers being gassed. They drowned in their own fluids as the noxious stuff ate away at their lung tissue. Finally, all the ice broke away. She fell to the floor, clutching her throat. Her lines were theatrical coughing.

"What is this?" he asked. "What are you, a fish plucked from an aquarium?"

Ramona stopped acting and sat up. "I was a soldier dying from a gas attack."

"Do you mean flatulence, because you're stinking this place up," he said. "I've seen enough. Stay there; I'm going to kill the lights."

The puppets quit moving. She heard Guy hurrying through the auditorium. She dug into her pocket for her phone and then texted Misty again.

No sooner had she hit the send button than a phone beeped. It sounded like Misty's—an unique sci-fi message tone. Ramona texted again. The tone sounded from behind the curtain.

The spots went out. The silhouetted puppets went away. The smell remained. Now she recognized it. The odor smelled like the stuff that had preserved dissection animals in high school biology. Ramona knew Guy would show up any minute. One more text confirmed that Misty's phone was behind the curtain. Ramona reached down and pulled it up from the bottom. The smell wafted out in a huge wave.

She held her breath and used her cell phone as a flashlight. The place filled with the eerie green glow. Pierced by large hooks on metal cables, the puppets hung lifeless. The fat Natalie O'Nell stared with bulging, dead eyes. Her tongue protruded from her mouth. Several other young women hung dead above the stage. Their limbs held up like marionettes. Then she saw Misty. Dried blood streaked her arms.

"I told you not to look behind the curtain," Guy said.

Ramona let the curtain fall. The director stood behind her with his arms crossed and a stern look carved on his face.

"I heard my friend's phone."

"You found her too, didn't you? I told you she got the part. Despite my first decision, it looks like you did as well."

She had no time to scream. Guy plunged a knife into her side. It slide perfectly between her ribs and into her heart. Ramona died staring up at the white stage curtain that she should never have looked behind.

***

Brad shook hands with Guy. A strong smell that burnt his nose ruined the beauty of the old restored theater. It made him a little nauseous.

"I had a friend audition yesterday. Her name was Ramona," Brad said. "I haven't heard from her."

"I remember her," Guy said. "She got the part despite her horrible audition. Let's see how you do."

Guy escorted Brad to the stage.

Blue Day

Steve finished a referral to child psychiatric services for the third crisis consult of the day. Three crises on a blue day, the one day per week a counselor had to see nothing but crises, was unusual. He'd usually sit all day twiddling his thumbs—bored. He hated blue days.

"Steve," a nasally voice cracked over the intercom in the telephone. "A deputy's just brought in a guy he picked up. I think you need to assess him."

"What's his story?"

"The deputy picked him up on Highway 119 and says he's a known drug addict."

"Send him to substance abuse," Steve said, looking up.

"That's not the reason he got picked up. He's really dirty and says a zombie attacked him."

"Send him back," Steve set his notes aside.

Steve liked delusionals because of their great stories. A tap came at his door. A large man in a brown uniform escorted in a skinny man dressed in a ratty, mud-stained T-shirt. The smell of wet dog, onions and reefer filled the room as the man sat on the vinyl chair near the window. He covered part of his right forearm with his hand. Steve reached into his desk drawer, and rubbed his finger in a jar of Vick's Vaporub. He pretended to scratch his nose so he could rub the salve underneath it. The fumes from the pungent stuff blocked all other smells.

"So what's happening?" Steve asked.

"This guy flagged me down and told me a zombie attacked him in Fike's Creek Cemetery," the deputy said.

Steve turned to the man. "What's your name?"

"Charlie."

"What are you covering with your hand?"

"Zombie bite. Didn't you hear what the deputy told you?"

Steve suppressed his anger. "Let me see it."

Charlie uncovered his forearm. He had a blood-crusted sore midway up his forearm. He covered it back up. His face twitched, and he scratched his chin with his shoulder.

"That's a mean-looking sore. Are you sure you didn't make that yourself?"

"No, I was bitten by a zombie. I ain't no nut!"

"Do you mean a zombie, like someone spaced out on drugs?"

"No, like a creeping around dead guy, hungry for human flesh!"

Steve waved his hands to calm Charlie down. "We don't have too many zombies attacking people up at Fike's Creek. Why were you there, anyway?"

"My mother's buried there. I went to see her."

"How did the zombie get there?" Steve asked.

"I guess he tore up through the ground," Charlie said more agitated.

The deputy snickered. Steve glanced up at him.

"Officer, I can handle this, if you need to get back to work."

The deputy nodded and walked out. Steve closed the door. He looked back at Charlie, who had tears in his eyes. Steve handed him a box of Kleenex. He took one and dabbed his eyes.

"You've got to believe me," Charlie said.

"I think you've been injured. I know you have. Do you have any psychiatric history in your family?"

"My mother died in River Bend. She had schizophrenia."

"Have you ever been bothered by voices or seen things?" Steve asked.

"No! I ain't no nut!"

"I'm not saying that you are. I'm just asking some questions." Steve tried to keep his voice calm. "Have you ever done drugs?"

"This is stupid," Charlie said. "I need to get this bite sanitized or something. It's like I'm being stung by a hundred wasps."

"I don't think there's a shot for zombie cooties," Steve said.

"Very freakin' funny. Why don't you drive out to that graveyard and let them gnaw on your arm for a while?"

"So there is more than one zombie?"

"There were three of them, I think; two guys and a chick. One of the guys bit me."

"Let me tell you what, I'm going to get our doctor and nurse to come take a look at that bite for you."

Steve left the room. He walked down the hall and found Dr. Ahad playing a card game on her computer. He rapped on the door.

"I'm sorry to bother you, but I need you to look at this crisis in my office. He has a big sore on his arm and claims a zombie bit him. Can you call Joan and have her meet us in my office?"

"I haven't seen a zombie attack in a while. I'd be glad to look at it," Dr. Ahad said. She called the nurse from the intercom and asked her to meet them.

Steve and Dr. Ahad walked into his office. Charlie still sat in the chair, jerking around and scratching his chin on his shoulder. Joan, the nurse, walked in with her first-aid kit and two syringes. One filled with Haldol, the other with

Ativan and an anti-side effect medication. Charlie looked at them. Steve noticed sweat on his brow and upper lip. His eyes looked red and bloodshot.

"Charlie, this is Dr. Ahad and our nurse," Steve said.

"You don't look so good," the doctor said in her sweet I-care-about-you voice.

"A zombie bit me, and that moron won't believe me."

"Show me the bite," the doctor said.

Charlie moved his hand. The blood-crusted wound again was swollen and red but looked like a human bite. Doctor Ahad nodded for the nurse to clean it. Joan washed away the gunk and scabby blood with alcohol. Charlie winced as it dripped into the raw parts of the wound. Dr. Ahad slid her glasses to the end of her nose and studied the wound.

"How did you get this to stop bleeding? I would think it would take a few stitches," Dr. Ahad said.

"It gummed up almost as soon as it happened," Charlie said. "It burns so bad."

"Why did you bite a plug out of your arm, Charlie?" the doctor asked.

"It was a zombie!"

"How many drugs have you done today?" she pressed.

"An eight-ball of crank and a couple of doobies," Charlie said.

"That's a lot of meth," Steve said. "How long have you been tweaking?"

"About three days," Charlie said.

"He is hallucinating from lack of sleep due to excessive drug use," Dr. Ahad told the nurse. "Call River Bend and tell them we're sending him down for detox and to get his wound sewn up."

"I'm not crazy!"

Charlie slung his good arm at Steve, knocking him aside. He shot up and moved toward the doctor. Steve steadied himself and grabbed Charlie in the restraining hold he had been taught several times but never used.

"Don't you get it? I'm not nuts!"

"Give him the cocktail," Dr. Ahad told the nurse.

Joan pulled the syringes out of her scrub's pocket and pushed them into Charlie's shoulder through his shirt. He struggled then stopped. Steve eased him down in the chair.

"Why won't you believe me," Charlie wailed. "This ain't meth. It was a freakin' zombie. There'll be more, man."

Charlie's head lulled, and his eyes focused on something in the distance.

"Steve, load him up and take him to the hospital. He's insane and not suitable for society," Dr. Ahad said.

"He's pretty rowdy. Maybe we could get the deputy—

"That would require a commitment. This way it's voluntary." Dr. Ahad turned to Charlie. "You want help, don't you?"

"Uh huh," he groaned.

"You see; he's willing."

***

Steve tossed the rearview mirror into the passenger-side seat as he drove the company's rattletrap Ford Taurus wagon south. He had tried to adjust it so he could watch Charlie in the backseat, but it fell off in his hand. The hospital was forty-five minutes away. Charlie would remain sedated until then. The car sputtered and backfired. After the last budget cuts from the state, the mental health center kept their old fleet of cars running on bubblegum and shoestrings. Sometimes they ran on just bubblegum at the end of the month when the funds were extra tight.

"This thing's a death trap," Steve told Charlie without looking back.

Charlie only grunted. Water splashed on the windshield. As it began to rain, Steve flipped on the wipers. They streaked the water across but didn't siphon it off. Steve slowed as he approached the cutoff road that led to Highway 119. He could drive slower on that road because of the smaller amount of traffic. He turned up the cutoff. Two miles later, he turned south onto Highway 119. He glanced at Charlie, who stared back with glazed eyes.

"Think we'll see that zombie that bit you?"

Charlie groaned.

Steve turned on the radio, searching the channels until he found the news. He caught a story about the nuclear plant upriver dumping radioactive material into the creek. Steve wondered if Charlie had been swimming and had radiation poisoning of some kind. He thought it might explain the coagulating of the blood around the wound.

"You didn't go swimming, did you?"

"Uh," Charlie groaned and thrashed against the seat belt.

"Settle down. We'll be there soon. They'll help you there."

The car passed over an iron bridge that crossed Fike's Creek. Steve looked up as they passed the flint-rock road that led to the cemetery. No zombies in sight, but maybe he could find out what had happened to Charlie. He pulled the car up the road to the cemetery. The road circled a knoll covered with gravestones blackened with lichen. Steve stopped where the bank slid into the creek and climbed out of the car. He left it running so that the air conditioning would keep Charlie cool and calm. Any other time, he would never imagine leaving a patient alone in a running car, but Charlie didn't know he was in the world. The Haldol cocktail worked miracles.

Steve didn't like this graveyard. He'd been here once before to assess a man named James who was living in the cemetery. The roots of the cedars in the middle had pushed some of the older headstones up at strange angles. Steve had a partner then, which made the hill a little less creepy. He had sent James to River Bend ages ago, but he had the feeling that he was being watched. Steve looked back at the car to see if Charlie was staring at him, but his head lolled on his chest.

Turning back to the creek, Steve stepped out where the bank sloped down. The ground was slick and muddy except for ruts where someone had climbed up from the water. The dark brown mud matched the stains on Charlie's shirt.

"I guess he did go for a swim," he said aloud.

He walked back to the car, watching the ground to keep from stumbling over a foot marker or an old discarded flowerpot. He looked up. Charlie pressed his face against the window. His red eyes glared out unblinking. Steve stopped short with a shudder. Charlie's head drooped again. Steve caught his breath, made it to the car and continued the drive. Gravel popped under the wheels, and a few pinged the undercarriage.

"I didn't find any zombies, but I see where you had been in the water," he said over his shoulder. "You've probably got radiation poisoning or something."

"No, zombie," Charlie drawled out.

"That's right, no zombie," Steve said, still looking back.

The gravel crackled as the car eased around the cemetery. The rain fell just enough to cast a foggy light over everything. Steve glanced at the tombstones he had been trying to avoid looking at. Underneath the gray cedars among the old gravestones that jutted everywhere like jack o'lantern teeth, a man stalked around, stumbling and holding his hands up to the sky. The position of the car made it hard to see anything else.

Maybe James was back and had quit taking his medications. He let the car move to a bend that divided the old part of the cemetery from the newer graves. From this angle Steve could tell the man was not James. The stranger's clothes were tattered and dirty, and his eyes grew wide when they focused on the car.

"I think I better call someone about that guy. He doesn't look so good," Steve said to Charlie, mostly to calm himself down.

"No … zombie…"

"I told you there was not a zombie down by the creek."

Steve watched the strange man as he crept toward the car. He suddenly had a thought. Charlie never said he went into the water, and he wasn't wet when he came into the office.

"Charlie, where is your mother's grave?"

"There."

Steve glanced over to see Charlie staring wide-eyed at him, but pointing to the right-hand side of the car. He followed the finger.

Steve screamed.

Another man pressed his face against the passenger-side window. He pawed at the glass, staring with eyes so wide Steve expected the eyeballs pop from their sockets. The man growled and licked the glass. Steve's foot slammed onto the gas pedal. The car tossed dirt and stone as it accelerated around the bend. In the side-view mirror, the man who had been pawing at the window lurched behind them.

"What the hell's going on?!" Steve asked.

"Zombies," Charlie growled, "hungry." He thrashed at the seatbelt. Steve had trouble steering around another curve, fighting to keep the tires on the road. One wrong move, and the car would roll down the embankment into the small hollow between the cemetery and the highway.

"Stop it, Charlie! I'm getting us out of here!"

The car jerked. Something flew up the windshield and over the roof. Steve slammed on the brakes. The car slid on the gravel pulling to the right. When the motion ceased, he looked behind him. A woman with long, stringy hair and sallow skin stood up behind the car. Her eyes were wide, and her left arm hung limply to the side. She reached out with the other and walked toward the car.

"What's the deal?" Steve asked again.

"Hungry." Charlie rattled the seat belt again.

"Will you stop that?"

"No."

Charlie's cold, clammy hand gripped his ear. Steve tried to spin around, but the grip was too tight. A searing pain tore across the top of his ear. It traveled down cartilage like a zipper sliding down. It took a moment for Steve to realize his ear ripped from his head. When the pain hit full force, it was like a hammer hit to the temple. A flash of agony shot through his head. The heady coppery smell of blood filled is nostrils as a sickening warmth ran down the side of his neck. His foot pegged the gas. The car jumped forward and then down the embankment. It jarred up and slammed down. Steve's dangling ear radiated pain down his whole side. The car headed for a large oak. He hit the brakes, but the front end slammed into the tree. Glass shattered. The hood buckled as the front end crunched in. The air bag hit Steve in the face, and Charlie's head gave a sickening crunch as it cracked against the windshield. He must have figured out how to release his seatbelt.

It was over. Steve looked up from the airbag. Stars danced before him, making Charlie's lifeless body appear to sparkle as it lay crumpled beside him. Pain coursed through his body, and more warm blood oozed down his face. A noise in the smoke-filled car made his heart stop. Charlie shifted and moaned. Steve unfastened his seat belt and fumbled with the door. It wouldn't budge. Charlie's fingers clutched at the air, and he groaned something that sounded like "brains." Steve tried to rationalize it but had no time. He pushed with all his force, freeing himself from behind the steering wheel. He slid out of the burst driver's window. Shards of glass cut his torso.

He fell to the ground but didn't feel it. Too much adrenaline pumped through is body. Getting to his feet, Steve climbed up the embankment toward the gravel drive. The wet leaves slipped from beneath his feet, and he slid back down to the car. Charlie crawled out of the driver-side window. His eyeball hung from the smashed left side of his face. He lurched toward Steve, who tried to claw his way up but slid down again.

"Someone help me! I'm being attacked by—zombies!"

Steve clambered back up the slope. Charlie grabbed his leg and jerked him down.

"Told you I wasn't nuts," Charlie moaned.

The zombie sank his teeth into Steve's leg. The undead venom burned as it entered his blood stream. Steve's body shut down. He couldn't feel his legs, and the numbness crept toward his brain. As it got to his head, he thought about how much he hated blue days.

Another Lost Boy

A rainbow of whirling lights flickered in Jonas' big blue eyes. Trick had forgotten how much fun it was to be a kid at the county fair. There weren't many other thrills in their backwoods part of Alabama. Trick felt that every 8-year-boy deserved to experience the same giddy sensation of all those folks from every walk of life thrown together to look at prize livestock and wait for the Tilt-a-whirl. The colored lights reflecting back to him in his son's wide eyes made him wish he were eight again too.

"So what do you want to do first?" he asked Jonas as they stepped through the main entrance turnstile.

The boy gazed over the midway at all the games that could be hustled by a carnie, from the ring toss to the dart-the-balloon booth. A Ferris wheel towered above them on one side. A short track roller coaster matched it on the other. The Tilt-a-whirl and Scrambler flanked the midway as well. Fake lightning flashed from the spook house, and raucous metal tunes from the 1980s filled the night with noise. The swinging pirate ship ended it all. For a moment, Jonas' head swept back and forth as he watched the ship swing to its apex and pendulum the other way.

To be eight and at the fair again! Trick picked up his nickname at a fair almost like this one when he was the same age as Jonas. He and his buddies had been playing the target-shooting game. The carnie asked his name, and he told him Patrick. Then he won the biggest, most expensive prize a kid could imagine, a giant foam sombrero, mostly by luck. That carnie said that he should be called Trick for the fast one he pulled on him. At the time, he hadn't understood what the guy meant, but now, many years later, he got it and liked that the moniker had stuck. His son wouldn't get such a cool name. Maybe he'd get Jona or Joe. He certainly hoped he didn't get pegged with Joan-ass. Trick was terrified his boy would go through life with that nickname; after all, kids can be cruel. But so far, none of his son's classmates had come up with this derivation yet.

"I don't know. What do you think, Daddy?"

"When we went to Six Flags last year, you really liked the roller coasters. We could try that one."

Jonas eyed the ride, cocking his head to one side. "Looks a little bit wussy."

"Wussy, huh? How about the Ferris wheel?"

His son dismissed the ride without even a look. "For girls."

Trick chuckled to himself. Maybe the kids *had* called him Joan-ass, and he'd shove it back to them. He put his hand on his son's shoulder and started walking down the midway. They passed the target-shooting booth and then the ring toss. Jonas looked from side to side trying to pick out what he wanted to do first. The spook house came up after the dart-a-balloon booth. Jonas stopped and studied the façade. Trick watched his son trace the outline of the large skull that marked the entrance to the ride with his eyes. He looked to the other side. A house of mirrors flanked the spook house. The boy's eyes lit up brighter than the bulbs flashing on the carousal. The choice was made. Only the verbal commitment waited.

"I want to do that first."

Deal negotiated, vocalized and agreed upon. Trick nodded his approval, and they stepped across the dusty path to the ticket booth. They brushed past a group of teenagers in black concert T-shirts who made an under-the-breath comment about how the old geezer needed to watch himself. Trick was about to give them the finger without Jonas seeing him, but he didn't have to; his son had already done it. Trick acted like he hadn't seen it. He loved that boy of his.

The ticket booth was covered with broken mirror shards. Each little sliver reflected all the spectacle of the fair, like staring into the multiple eyes of a giant spider. Trick hated spiders. Despite the excitement of the carnival attraction and the secret pride of seeing his son flip off a bunch of punks, for some reason he felt an awful dread about the house of mirrors.

The man running the booth wore a star-spangled bandana around his head. His moustache was full like a walrus, but his scraggly beard had several days of unshaven growth. He smiled, the single bulb illuminating the booth showing off the yellow shade of his teeth. He eyed Trick and Jonas warily as they approached.

"Ten tickets," he said.

"We've got these." Jonas shoved his wrist toward the carnie. A lime green, paper bracelet hung loosely from his arm.

After Trick showed his, the carnie nodded his head toward the door. Jonas tugged on Trick's hand to hurry, but he stayed in place staring at the gaping maw of an entryway. Strips of heavy black plastic covered the door, making it impossible to see inside. Trick looked back at the carnie ticket taker.

"What's the problem, Bud? I told you to go on."

"Is this a maze or just a bunch of trick mirrors that make you look short and fat or tall and skinny?" Trick asked.

"A little bit of A, a little bit of B."

Nodding, Trick allowed his son to pull him to the opening of the maze. A set of rusty metal steps led up to the opening, and Jonas sprang up them first, the steps shaking from side to side underfoot as they ascended. Trick put his hand on Jonas' shoulder before the boy could slip inside.

"Listen, this place is a maze of mirrors so it's going to be real easy to get lost. Let's stick together just in case that happens."

"All right, Daddy."

Jonas pushed through the plastic strips, and Trick followed. Hot air greeted him. Little beads of sweat popped up on his forehead near his hairline as soon as he walked in; the whole place felt like a swamp in summer. The heat didn't seem to affect Jonas one bit as he ran straight to a wavy mirror against the side wall. Trick stood beside him, staring at their odd reflections. He looked like someone had pushed a large amount of his mass into his hips and butt and stretched him thin above the waist, sending those leftovers to his forehead. Jonas appeared more alien, the majority of his body squat and bulbous, except his head. It stretched up long, with his eyes taking up a large portion of this space.

"Come on, Daddy. Let's see what this one does." He moved to the next mirror.

Trick stepped to it. Now they both looked like NBA players, long and lean. Jonas giggled and moved to the next mirror. The anxiety that had knotted inside of Trick's guts let up a bit.

"You've got to see this one, Patty."

"What did you call me?"

"I called you Daddy. I said, 'you've got to see this one, Daddy.'"

He could have sworn his son had called him Patty, a nickname that died the day he beat the game at the carnival and won the moniker Trick so many years ago. The next mirror did something remarkable. Although Jonas stood beside him, Trick only saw himself, but more than that. He was 8-years-old again.

"It's great, isn't it?" Jonas asked.

"I don't know. What do you see?"

"My face is all squeezed in like my head's been squished. Watch this." He stuck his tongue out.

Trick saw his son do this in the mirror now. Sure enough, Jonas looked like his head was squeezed together. His own now-adult image did the same, yet his feeling of apprehension returned when they moved to the last joke mirror, after which came the maze. A neon sign with some of the lettering burned out hung over another door made from strips of black plastic. He turned to look into the last mirror. Again he was 8-years-old and wearing a huge foam sombrero. He'd won it the day he earned the better nickname. Billy O'Rear stood beside him in the mirror making monkey faces.

The mirror's effect made them all look a little apish. Sam Costello poked his head between the two boys to get a gander. Danny Tidmore hopped above them to do the same thing. All the boys laughed and cut up except for Trick.

"What's going on, son?" Trick asked, caught between the real world and his memories.

"Son?" Billy said. "Just because you're wearing a big hat doesn't mean that you can call me son."

Trick ripped the sombrero off his head and tossed it down. Then Trick, once called Patty, shoved Billy.

"Why are you acting so funny, Patty?" Danny asked.

"It's Trick," Sam said. "We ain't calling him Patty anymore."

"This isn't right. I'm a 37-year-old man, not eight."

"Don't have a cow, man," Danny said and then snorted a laugh.

"D'oh!" Sam slapped himself on the head.

Billy pulled away. "Quit goofing off, Trick. I want to get through this thing so we can go to the spook house."

He ran into the maze. Danny and Sam followed. Trick watched them go, wanting to scream to the top of his lungs. Someone tugged on his arm. He looked down and was startled to see Jonas staring up at him.

"Are you okay, Daddy?"

Trick felt like he'd just awakened from a dream. He rubbed his forehead and smiled down at his son reassuringly. "Just had a moment."

"Brain fart?"

"I guess you could call it that. Are you ready to get this over with? I want to go ride the Scrambler. I think you'll love it."

"Am I ever!" Jonas hurried to the flaps. He reached out for Trick. "We need to stay together, remember."

The air felt ten degrees cooler in the maze. Somewhere deep in the reflective labyrinth an air conditioner hummed overhead. Jonas stood at the entryway. His gaped mouth reflected back to Trick in numerous mirrors. It was an almost comic effect. He wanted to chuckle, but something cold prickled inside the pit of his stomach. Déjà vu always felt uncanny, but this feeling was like a cold punch to the gut, enough to force the air out of his lungs. Trick had been in this place before. Deep in the forgotten regions of memory, something about the mirror maze poked at him like shards of glass. Something else held those memories below the surface. He stared a long time into the mirrors lining the entrance to the maze, even after his son's expression of awe faded into one of frustrated anticipation.

"Come on, Daddy. We're wasting time, and you said you wanted to go on the Scribbler."

"Scrambler, like eggs," he corrected, not paying much attention to the words that fell out of his mouth as if he couldn't close his lips.

Jonas tugged on his arm, and Trick entered the darkness of the mirror maze. A strange feeling of disorientation hit him as soon as they crossed into the labyrinth. Seven Jonases stood in front of seven reversed versions of himself. He turned around to find the door back to the entrance, but reflections stared back at him when he did. The whole place turned and twisted like glass vertigo.

"Which way do we go?" Jonas asked. "All I see is us."

"That's what makes these things so hard." Trick closed his eyes hoping that opening them would clear up all the clones, and he could see the next turn.

"And fun?"

He opened his eyes. Sure enough the space between two mirrors on the wall became obvious. "Some folks think so." He pointed. "That way."

Jonas tiptoed through the opening as if he were afraid he would hit a mirror. Trick smiled and followed behind his son. The echo of a memory swirled inside his head. He could practically hear a much younger version of himself saying the same words when he'd just transitioned from being Patty to Trick. As the memory came back to him, he remembered having a lot more fun that time.

It had been Halloween. They all wore costumes. He was Slimer but had left the rigid plastic mask in his parents' car. It was too uncomfortable for playing at the fair, but he still wore the plastic smock with the character's body printed on it on.

The cool air in the mirror maze felt good because the plastic costume didn't breathe much. The big sombrero he'd been wearing made him almost as hot as the Slimer mask. Sweat plastered his hair to his forehead.

Billy held the edges of his black vampire cape and flapped his arms up and down. The cape had been his whole costume. He wore it over his school clothes. *The Lost Boys* was his favorite movie. He'd believed no one would get that he was just a kid who was also a vampire, so he added the cape.

Danny wore blue shorts, a red T-shirt, and his hair spiked up. Sam, as always, was a cowboy, but not any old cowboy, Clint Eastwood from *The Good, the Bad, and the Ugly*. A rolled up piece of brown construction paper served as his cigar. Smears of his mother's dark brown eye shadow made his stubble beard.

In the dim light of the maze, each boy stared at himself in the mirrors. Trick felt stupid in his store-bought, el cheapo costume. He'd never been very original in his ideas. Painting his face green and wearing a green shirt and pants could have implied Slimer, or the Hulk. Both would have been cool. He pulled at the plastic costume.

"Quit fooling with that, dude," Danny said, trying his best to sound like Bart Simpson.

"I wish I'd just done something different," Trick admitted.

"You did. You totally won at that game," Danny replied, shrugging his shoulders. "So you got on some stupid plastic costume—we racked up on candy."

Trick had forgotten about that. Everything looked up a bit. He decided to lead the way into the maze. Everything seemed unreal as he walked into the next hall, like walking through a mirror. His mother used to read him the story of Alice going through the looking glass.

"Come on, guys," he yelled back to his friends.

"Don't have a cow, man!" Another bad Bart Simpson impression.

They all laughed, though, because *The Simpsons* was the greatest show ever, even if he had to sneak and watch it because his mom thought it was unfit for kids.

The lighting in this hallway was dimmer, causing their reflections to scarcely look more than ghostly shadows instead of four 8-year-old boys. Two gaps opened up in this hall.

"Which way?" Sam asked.

"We could split up. Two go this way and two the other," Billy suggested.

None of them looked like they were keen on the idea of splitting up. Trick certainly wasn't. The other's might need the spook house for creeps and scares, but the unnerving feeling building in his stomach was more than sufficient.

"I think we should just go that way." Danny pointed to the opening with the least amount of light. "They probably try to trick people to take the wrong way by lighting it better."

The boys agreed that this sounded like good logic and followed the dark path. Although he'd charged forward the first time, Trick brought up the rear just in case something jumped out at them on their way through. This section of the maze seemed to go on forever, as a seemingly endless line of mirrors led them straight ahead. The mirrors on the right wall were offset, not quite lining up to those on the left so that strange going-on-forever effect didn't occur. Trick liked that because he'd always felt like he saw someone walking up from the very depth of the endless reflection.

Danny, who walked birddog, stopped and turned around, his face solemn. "Dead end."

Billy looked from side to side. "Here's a door."

He slipped between two mirrors. Danny and Sam followed. Trick stopped and looked into the dead-end wall. Tiny lines spider-webbed across the reflective glass, but they weren't large enough or numerous enough to obscure the reflection. He stared deep into the glass. Just at the point that he lost focus, something moved. He cut his eyes to that section of the mirror, but only his slightly scared face looked back. Trick walked toward the opening without taking his eyes off that spot. The edge of the opening hit him hard between the shoulders. Air expelled from his lungs in a startled gasp.

"What's the matter, Daddy?"

Trick blinked hard and realized that he'd rammed his knee into the edge of an opening as he and Jonas passed through.

"Hit my knee. I guess I wasn't paying too much attention."

"You need to be careful. If you break one of these things, you'll get cut all to pieces."

He smiled at his son. It was one of those sarcastic smiles that parents use when their child has been patronizing, intentionally or not.

"Thank you, mother. I'll be more careful."

Trick supposed he was being silly. Childhood figments of the imagination shouldn't be causing him such anxiety. It was just like when he stayed in hotels with shower curtains—he always kept his back to the stall wall expecting a crossdresser with a knife to come after him; even though the last time he'd watched that movie he was 13-years-old. Childhood fears, much to his chagrin, were larger than life and died hard.

He and Jonas came to a dead end. He stared at their reflection in the mirror, and just at the edge of his vision, he saw something shadowy move.

Trick hated feeling like a scared kid, but when he walked into the next stretch of maze that sense of childish helplessness almost overwhelmed him. The mirrors lined up across from one another forming a never-ending cascade of reflections. Jonas stood as close to one of them as he could without pressing his face to the glass. Trick wanted to pull him back as quickly as possible, but hesitated. His son had never seen something like this. He'd let him stare into the terrifying infinity for just a few moments longer.

"Get a look at this, Daddy. It's crazy."

"I've seen it before."

"It looks like it could go on forever and ever."

"It's just an illusion caused by the mirrors being lined up in the right way."

"It's still totally cool," Billy said.

Trick wished that his repressed memories would stay where they belonged. The switching back and forth from present to daydream gave him worse vertigo than the mirror maze. Instead of his son leaning against the wall of mirrors, his friend, Billy the Lost Boy, pressed his hands against one of them. The others gawked into them as well.

"It's like if you push hard enough, you might just fall through into that long hallway," Billy said.

"This reminds me of that music video where the guy bounces back and forth between being a cartoon and a real person," Danny said.

Sam started bouncing between mirrors. He didn't hit them hard enough with his shoulders to do anything but make them all laugh. Billy started doing the same thing, and before long they all joined in. Trick flung his shoulder into a mirror. Nothing caught him, and he lost his balance, toppling into the next stretch of the maze. The clatter from the metal grate flooring echoed through the maze when he landed on his side. Sam, Billy, and Danny stepped through the gap, laughing harder than ever.

"Trick, you are some kind of klutz," Danny exclaimed, reaching down to offer him his hand.

He took advantage of it and pulled against his friend until he was on his feet. This stretch of mirror hallway formed nothing but the infinite reflections, like millions of evil eyes staring at him. For the first time all night, Trick felt more than a little bit scared.

"This part's a bit creepy," Sam whispered, which made Trick happy.

"Let's get through it quick," Trick said.

He and Sam hurried down the straightaway. Danny came up from behind him not leaving much space between them. Billy, however, kept humming that Aha tune, and mocked bouncing between the mirrors. He could always be a little bit annoying. The maze opened into another wide room. The three boys stopped and watched Billy creep through it. He insisted on tapping each mirror with his shoulder.

"You boys are sissies," Billy hit the last mirror on the right and ricocheted off to the left. That's when Trick saw his best friend fall into the mirror. His blue, canvas sneakers flew up in the air like something out of a cartoon. Billy hollered as his feet passed across the threshold into the mirror.

Trick suddenly grabbed Jonas by the shoulders and pulled him back from the mirror.

"Don't lean up against that, son."

"Why not?" his son asked.

"It might not be bolted down good. I wouldn't want it to fall over and break. You'd get cut to pieces."

"Daddy, you worry too much."

Trick didn't think so. Billy had slipped through that mirror—he'd seen it himself. Only ... had he? There was no way his best childhood friend could have fallen into a mirror. He had to be remembering a nightmare or some movie plot. It had happened once before. At work one day, Trick had told some of the guys how he and those same three friends set out across the woods to find the dead body of a boy hit by a train. After describing what had happened for a few minutes, one of his coworkers had interrupted to tell him that sounded a lot like the movie *Stand by Me*. He'd not seen it since he was 12 or 13, but when he reflected back on it; he had mistaken it for his own life. That was what this daydream had to be. Billy had moved away to Mobile, not long after that Halloween excursion to the fair. Trick put his hand on his son's shoulder.

"Let's keep going. I really want to ride the Scrambler."

"Okay—race!"

Jonas took off running through the dimly lit maze. Trick tried to snag his son by the collar, but the boy was too quick, and evaded his grasp. He didn't waste his breath calling after Jonas. Instead, Trick trotted after him. He didn't sprint for fear of colliding into someone else in the maze.

The hall took a sharp turn. He banged his elbow into one of the mirror walls while making the bend and slammed into a dead end. Several distorted versions of his reflection looked back at him, all of them having the same anxious look on their faces. The maze should have been called the Déjà vu. Ever since he'd stepped into the place that stupid French feeling threatened to stifle him. The whole place was like the twisting and turnings of his own memories, the machinations of his mind's inner labyrinth.

He headed in the opposite direction. The corridor made two sharp turns but kept going. He could hear the heavy footfalls of Jonas running somewhere ahead. Now panicking, Trick ran with his arm out to keep from slamming into the mirrors. His heart beat fast, much too fast for the effort he put forth.

"Where are you?" he shouted, feeling a sickly, coppery taste in his mouth.

His words echoed, but in other voices. Sam parroted exactly what he had said. Danny asked a slightly different version of the same question. But Billy's normally extroverted voice remained silent. They were trying to find him. They'd heard him yelp, but it was like he'd disappeared into one of the mirrors. The boys rounded a corner into a better lit section of maze. Trick sighed with relief as he glimpsed Billy running ahead of them, his black cape fluttering behind him.

"There he goes," Danny said.

"How did he get ahead of us?" Trick asked.

"He must have fallen into a secret shortcut or something," Danny guessed.

"Wait up!" Sam ordered.

Trick was ahead of the others. He ran harder. Billy continued to put distance between himself and them. The hallway couldn't have possibly been that long. Before he realized it, Trick slammed full body into a mirror. The impact knocked off his sombrero and bounced him backward onto the ground. His tailbone struck painfully on the metal floor. The other two boys helped him clamber to his feet. They stared into the mirror, watching Billy running off into the distance in an infinity of reflections. He never looked back. The boy in the vampire cape ran until all Trick could see was a tiny spot of black in the eternal tube of the mirror.

No one believed them when they'd told their parents and the police what had happened to Billy. Everyone said he'd been kidnapped by some carnie, and that the trauma was causing all three boys to share a common delusion. He'd not even thought about all that until right then, as he looked into a mirror and saw his 37-year-old face staring back.

"Where are you at, Jonas?" he yelled.

"Over here, Daddy."

Trick looked around, startled, and was relieved to see his son standing behind him. Relief washed over him; for a panicked moment between reality and flashback, he'd thought he'd lost Jonas in the never-ending reflective maze.

"Let's get out of here. I'm ready to do something else." He held his hand out to his son.

Jonas smiled and turned his back to him. "Let's go this way."

He watched his son run full speed down a long hall of mirrors that seemed to go on forever. The word *no* welled up inside him, but nothing came from his mouth except a tight, stiff yelp. Trick lunged at the mirror. His palm slammed into the smooth glass. He closed his fingers, hoping to grab ahold of his son's shirt, but his fist slid down the pane. Jonas ran farther and farther away, never looking back.

Rage billowed up within Trick the same way he'd felt so many years ago when Billy slipped away. Then, he'd been too young to know what to do. Now, he knew what would free his son. Trick reared back and kicked the mirror with all his might.

At the point of impact, the glass fractured into a spider-web of fissures. As he drew his foot back, small pieces fell to the floor, glittering in the poor light. Larger chunks broke off and hit the floor as the mirror crumbled from the wall. He waited for the shower of glittering glass to stop and his son to appear unharmed, but when the last of the shards rested on the metal floor, only the bare plywood remained. Trick looked down at the destroyed mirror.

Instead of setting of his son free, dozens if not hundreds of Jonases, ran through the never-ending hall of mirrors.

Trick looked over his shoulder back at the maze. It looked like he was in a long hallway that kept going until it ended in a black dot. That black dot sucked everything out of him at that moment, and he heard Billy giggling as the caped boy dashed through the mirrors in pursuit of his son, another lost boy.

Publication History

"A Cat Named Hercules" first published in *Hazard Yet Forward*, 2012

"Another Lost Boy" first published in *Dark Moon Digest 18*, 2015

"Best Offer" first published in *Dark Moon Digest 7*, 2012

"Blue Day" first published on the *Nocturnal Ooze* website, 2007

"Dry Places" first published in *The Literary Hatchet, special issue 9*, 2014

"New Orleans' Best Beignets" first published in *Help Wanted! Tales of on-the-job Terror*, 2011

"Pabst Blue Ribbon Moon" first published in *It was a Dark and Stormy Night...*, 2011

"Red Teeth" first published in *Dark Moon Digest 15*, 2014

"The Silver Needle" first published in *Side Show 2: Tales of the Big Top and the Bizarre*, 2010

Vic Kerry lives in Alabama with his wife, five dogs and a cat. He holds an MFA in writing popular fiction from Seton Hill University and an MS in clinical psychology from the University of South Alabama. He has published two novels: *The Children of Lot* and *Revels Ending*, a novella: *Decoration Day*, and numerous short stories. He spends his days working on a psychiatric unit and his nights dreaming up nightmares.

www.ingramcontent.com/pod-product-compliance
Lightning Source LLC
Chambersburg PA
CBHW032010180726
48283CB00008B/2608